A BEACH HOUSE TO DIE FOR

A COSTA RICA COZY MYSTERY

K.C. AMES

17th
STREET
BOOKS

ABOUT THIS BOOK

What could go wrong with starting over in a tropical paradise?

Life in San Francisco was getting too expensive, too hectic, and too crowded for recently divorced Dana Kirkpatrick.

When this big-city girl inherited a beach house in a coastal Costa Rica town, she took it as a sign and packed her bags.

Dana imagined the small beach town would have its challenges, but she never could have predicted legal troubles, local wildlife, and being adopted by a stray cat. And now she's suspected of murder!

It's not quite the fresh start she envisioned when she moved to the tropical paradise beach community of Mariposa Beach.

If you love quirky characters, offbeat animals, and small beach town charm with a cozy mystery to solve, then you will love this new series!

Although this is a series the books stand alone and you can read them in any order you like.

ONE

"You're moving to Costa Rica?" Courtney Lowe asked, mouth agape.

It was the reaction Dana Kirkpatrick expected after telling her best friend about her big decision.

"I've been talking about it for months."

"Well, yeah, I just never figured you would go from talking to actually moving," Courtney said, sounding incredulous.

"It finally feels right," she said, a thin smile poorly masking the nervousness of her decision.

Dana's stomach felt like it was Play-Doh being twisted and squeezed by an overactive child.

"Dana, you're my best friend, and I love you, but this..." she paused, and Dana could see her mulling over for the right words for a moment. *Bless her heart*, she didn't want to insult or be dismissive about her decision. "...doesn't it seem a bit too drastic of a move, so soon after Phil?"

Dana felt that Courtney wanted to take her by the shoulders and shake her out of whatever it was she felt that led her to make such a life-changing decision.

"Oh, please, you know me better than that. I'm not running

away because of Phil. *That* ship has long sailed away, and we've both moved on. It's the magic of divorce."

Courtney held her hands up in surrender. "But why there? In another country?"

"We've always talked about going to Costa Rica," Dana replied innocently.

Courtney rolled her eyes and tilted her head sideways and said, "Well, yeah, on vacation. For ten days, two weeks. Just enough time to enjoy the beaches, the tropical weather, do that jungle zip line thing, flirt with cute guys, and then come back home like good tourists do."

Dana tried to speak, but Courtney wasn't finished. "Moving there is a whole other song and dance."

Dana shrugged and said, "Home is where the heart is, and no offense to Tony Bennett, but my heart is no longer in San Francisco."

"And your heart is in Costa Rica? Come on, sweetie. You've only been there a few times."

"Once, actually," Dana replied.

"Once, wow. I stand corrected. And how long ago was that?"

"About ten years ago, but what does that matter?" Dana replied, becoming annoyed with the interrogation.

"Sorry, but don't you think it's nutty to move down there permanently, especially to such a remote part of the country and to such a small town? It would be a little different if you were at least moving to the capital. But your uncle's place is off the beaten path."

"That's the part that appeals to me the most, plus it's always warm and I would be right on the beach. Besides, San Francisco is too cold, too overcrowded, too expensive, downtown smells like a toilet, and for a bonus, I hate my job," Dana said.

"Don't hold back now."

"I love you and will miss you like crazy, but seriously, there is nothing to keep me here anymore."

"Just stick around a while. Let the ink dry on your divorce papers. If you want to do something drastic, lop off all your hair, get involved with a twenty-something-year-old. Isn't that a post-divorce thing to do?"

"I'll be thirty-five in a few months and I'm not interested in becoming Mrs. Robinson. And you know how long I've been growing it out, so why should I take it out on my poor hair? My hair is innocent," Dana said, running her hands through her brown hair. She started to laugh and Courtney joined in laughing, lightening the mood.

"I know you're worried about me and I appreciate it, but I feel now is the time to make a huge change in my life," Dana said to Courtney, and to herself, continuing, "everything has lined up perfectly." She counted down with her fingers, "The divorce is final, the house is sold and in escrow with fifty percent of that coming my way—thank you San Francisco tech bubble, part deux—then out of the blue, I find out I'm inheriting my uncle's beach house in Costa Rica, free and clear. I mean, come on, all signs point to go, *now*." Dana wiggled her three fingers in the air, driving the points home.

Courtney shrugged, then said, "Well, you're going to get so bored in a little beach town in the middle of nowhere, way down in Central America. I doubt they have high-powered PR firms down there."

"Good, I'm done with public relations."

"I'm sure you can go back to work as a journalist for the newspaper."

"Back to that dying business? No thanks. Besides, news organizations don't want journalists anymore. They want bloggers who can come up with clickbait headlines."

Courtney shrugged again. Dana smiled. She knew

Courtney had lost that argument. But she loved how much her friends cared about her.

"I'm excited about this, Court, and the time is right," Dana said, psyching herself back up again about her decision.

Courtney wrinkled her nose and twisted her mouth, reminding Dana of the McKayla Maroney *I'm not impressed* look.

She laughed again.

"It's not like I'm leaving tomorrow. I have to stick around as the legal mumbo jumbo with my uncle's estate and the sale of our house here gets sorted out. Besides, I'll be just a plane ride away."

TWO

Three months later, Dana was sitting in the back of a nine-seat, single-engine airplane over the skies of Costa Rica.

The turbulence made it bounce up and down in the air like it was a bingo ball bouncing around in a blower machine.

Courtney was sitting next to her. She had convinced her to make the trip down to help her get settled in and keep her company for a couple weeks as she got the lay of the land down in the tropics.

They sat elbow-to-elbow in the small airplane. Dana turned her head to see how Courtney was holding up from the bumpy ride. She couldn't help but laugh as Courtney was shooting eye daggers back at her.

Dana turned away and looked out the window. Below was the Costa Rican jungle, and on the horizon, like an oasis, the Pacific Ocean.

The plane kept shaking and dipping. Courtney clamped down on her hand and squeezed hard. Dana turned to her to comfort her, but she just mouthed off *I hate you*, which caused Dana to break out laughing. Courtney joined in.

The pilot, Walter Espinoza Jr., sat in the cockpit with both hands on the yoke, but he seemed as cool as a cucumber to Dana. *That's comforting*, she thought.

Captain Junior—"like Junior Soprano," he had explained to the passengers before takeoff—was the owner and only pilot of Tropic Air, which flew customers from the capital city of San José down to the coastal beaches.

He had handed out headsets to communicate during the flight.

Dana heard her headset crackle to life with the radio voice of Captain Junior saying, "No worries, this is the rough part I warned you about. From now on, it's all pura vida."

Dana had learned from her first trip to Costa Rica that "pura vida," Spanish for "pure life," was something of a national credo spoken by just about every Costa Rican man, woman, and child, regardless of age, economic standing, or background.

They used pura vida as a verb, adjective, and noun, and Dana believed there must be some local legal requirement for every living citizen in Costa Rica to say pura vida at least once a day.

"We'll be landing in a few minutes," Captain Junior said, much to their delight.

As bumpy and scary as the flight had been, the pilot expertly landed the plane smooth as butter.

"Welcome to Nosara," he said, his voice a crackle in Dana's headset.

Dana and Courtney looked out the window. It was a one-runway municipal airport without a control tower, and the terminal looked more like a baseball dugout than an airport terminal.

"Now that's one small airport," Dana said, removing the headset.

"I really don't care, I just want off this thing," Courtney

said. She removed her headset and began looking around impatiently until the plane finally stopped.

Once Captain Junior opened the door, Dana, Courtney, and the two other passengers on the flight exited the airplane like Seabiscuit from the gate.

They stood on the runway for a moment and sucked in the warm tropical air.

"Oh, that feels so good," Courtney said.

"The nice tropical air?" Dana asked.

"No, good old asphalt under my feet. I'm about to get on my knees like the Pope and kiss the ground. Next time, we drive."

"Saved us five hours in traffic, and believe me, Costa Rican driving is just as scary as that airplane."

Dana and Courtney made their way to the parking lot area with their rolling suitcases. They waved off a couple of taxi drivers as they walked towards a handsome man that was standing in front of a white Toyota Land Cruiser, waving at Dana.

Dana waved back. They had talked a lot over the phone and video chat the last couple months, but it was the first time they were meeting in person. Dana felt her heart pounding in her chest like a cartoon character.

THREE

His name was Benny Campos. He was Dana's Costa Rican lawyer, and he was handsome and a charmer to boot.

"Oh, my," Courtney whispered to Dana when she first laid eyes on him.

"Down, girl," Dana whispered back.

Thanks to video chat, she already knew how good-looking he was, but she hadn't shared that little nugget with Courtney, who had become bedazzled by the lawyer. Dana chuckled inwardly.

He was in his mid-thirties and had olive skin, with brown hair worn short and neatly styled. His eyes were also brown, with an amber hue to them.

"It's so nice to finally meet in person, Dana," Benny said as they shook hands. It was a professional, firm, all-business handshake.

"Likewise. We've spoken so much over Skype, I forgot we hadn't met in person."

There was an awkward silence for a second or two.

"I'm Courtney Lowe."

Dana blushed. "I'm sorry, how rude of me. This is my best friend; she'll be staying with me for a couple weeks."

"Excellent, it's good that you'll have a friend around to help you get settled in," Benny said. "How was the flight?" he quickly added.

"It was fine, with some scary parts here and there," Dana said.

"Hmm, it made me recall the safe travel prayer from my youth," Courtney said with a grin.

"I wish you would have let me pick you up at the airport in San José. I would have been more than happy to drive you both down to Casa Verde," Benny said.

"Casa Verde?" Courtney asked.

"It's a common thing in a lot of Latin American countries to give your home a name. Casa Verde is Spanish for Green House. When you see it, you'll see it's a most appropriate name, since the property is located in a lush tropical forest near the beach. And it's the name Blake Kirkpatrick gave to Dana's place," Benny explained.

Dana's place. She let those words sink it. It sounded surreal.

"Earth to Dana," Courtney said after another awkward silence.

Again, Dana was blushing. "Sorry, when you said Dana's place...I'm just not used to it yet, especially with all the weird legal drama going on."

Benny smiled. "Real estate is a full-contact sport in Costa Rica." He grabbed their suitcases and popped them in the back of his SUV.

Benny drove west from Nosara, turning into a tour guide.

"Nosara is the big town around these parts—population of around five thousand," he explained with a smile.

"Look, Dana, a yoga studio," Courtney said, pointing out the window at a sign written in English that was advertising Yoga and Spiritual Healing.

"Believe it or not, Nosara has become a major yoga hub worldwide. It has always been known as a first-class surf destination, but in the last couple decades, the yogis have taken over. Yoga teachers come from all over the world to learn from the gurus out here. There are also some great restaurants, coffee shops, even an organic market in town. The expats that have settled here are trying to turn it into a mini tropical Berkeley," Benny said, smiling.

"You've been to Berkeley, Benny?" Courtney asked.

"He went to law school at Hastings," Dana answered for him.

"Oh, you never told me that," Courtney said, sounding surprised.

"UC Tenderloin," Benny said, grinning. He was referring to his alma mater by its nickname for being in the nefarious, rough-and-tumble San Francisco neighborhood known as the Tenderloin.

"Small world," Courtney said.

"Dana's uncle wanted a local lawyer that also knew about California law. I'm a member of the Costa Rican and California bar. There aren't too many of us around."

"That explains why you speak English so well," Courtney said.

"My parents made sure I learned English at a very young age. They sent me to a bilingual school in San José to make sure I learned English well, since it's a very beneficial language to know from a business perspective. It comes in very handy now, since most of my clients are Americans and Canadians. And even the European clients all speak English, so that's the default language for communicating with most of the clients."

"So, what's Benny short for? Benjamin? Bernard?" Courtney asked.

Dana could see it in Benny's face that it was a question that had been asked a lot and that he still found it a tad bit embarrassing to answer.

"So you're wondering why a grown adult, an attorney, asks to be called Benny?"

Courtney fidgeted, hemming and hawing for a moment as Dana smiled widely. Courtney struggled, saying, "Well, no. I didn't mean to offend...um, insinuate."

Benny mercifully put her out of the awkward bind.

"I'm joking. Benny is my given name. My mother was a huge Elton John fan, and 'Benny and the Jets' was one of her favorite songs. So there you have it. I guess I could have gone with Ben, but I figured I would go with the name she gave me."

Dana hadn't heard that story, since she was not as big of a digger into people's personal lives as Courtney loved to be.

"Oh, wow, so you're named after an Elton John song?" Dana said. She could hardly finish saying it without laughing out loud.

"It could be worse. If your mother was into Johnny Cash, you could have been a boy named Sue," Dana said.

They all shared a laugh over the silliness as Dana shrugged and looked out the window at the brightly colored buildings and funky signs on the businesses and retail stores.

Courtney was also looking out the window, taking it all in. "It does have a Berkeley vibe here. And here you thought you were getting away from the Bay Area."

"We're headed to Playa Mariposa Azul, which means Blue Butterfly Beach in English. Everyone just calls it Mariposa Beach. Nice and short. Mariposa Beach is more secluded, but it's a wonderful, tight-knit beach community. More Santa Cruz than Berkeley," Benny explained.

"That's probably why my uncle fell in love with the area. He was a surfing hippie. He first came to Costa Rica in the seventies to surf," Dana said.

"He was a smart man. Bought land down here in the early eighties when it was dirt-cheap. It's now worth a princely sum," Benny said.

"Is it called Blue Butterfly Beach because there are a lot of blue butterflies down here?" Courtney asked.

"They named it after the morpho butterfly, but they are not commonly seen down by the beach. You usually have to go into the forest up in the mountains to find them, although now and then one of them might make it down to the beach, but I wouldn't hold my breath hoping to see one in town."

"Sounds like false advertisement to me, then," Courtney said as they all laughed.

To Dana, the drive down to Mariposa Beach seemed bumpier than the flight down. As they pulled into town, Benny asked if they were hungry.

"Starving," Courtney replied.

"Me too."

"There is a great place to eat in town. It's nothing fancy, but they serve excellent typical tico food at tico prices," Benny said.

"Sounds fantastic," Dana said.

"So what's the deal with that word, tico? I hear it all the time. At first, I thought it was a derogatory slur against Costa Ricans, but Dana tells me it's not."

"Not at all. After pura vida, *tico* is a word you will hear a lot from the locals," Benny explained.

"Where did that word come from, and what does it mean, exactly?" Dana asked.

"Well, it's a made-up word, really; it has been around forever, way before my time. I guess *Costarricense* sounded too formal and proper. Supposedly, the word originated from our predilection to add a diminutive suffix to everything we say. For example, it's not chiquito, but chiquitito; it's not amor, but amorcito. Who knows the saying's true genesis, but everyone uses it."

They parked at Soda Linda. Benny had explained that a soda in Costa Rica was like a cafe or diner in the states. And like a diner back in the states, Soda Linda offered counter service, meaning you sat at the counter to order and eat your meal. It was open air, and they didn't have tables, just nine stools at the counter.

"Place is small," Dana said as she looked around.

"During breakfast, lunch, and dinnertime, there can be a long line, and forget about finding a spot at the counter. You get your food to go. Lucky for us it's two in the afternoon, so we can even sit together," Benny said, sitting down on one of the stools. Dana and Courtney did the same.

"Hey Benny, who are your friends?" the woman on the other side of the counter said with a smile.

Benny introduced them to Linda Orozco, the owner.

"Oh, you're the Linda from Soda Linda," Dana said, smiling.

"That's me, and you must be Blake Kirkpatrick's niece. Nice to meet you."

The place had a limited menu. Its specialty was the casado, which was a typical Costa Rican dish that consisted of a mélange of rice, beans, plantains, salad, and chicken, beef, or fish. Benny ordered the casado with steak.

"What did my uncle like to eat?"

Linda smiled. "The fish casado was his favorite."

"I'll have that, then."

"And I'll have the chicken one just to be different," Courtney said.

For a beverage, Benny ordered a fresco de cas.

He explained, "We're known for our tropical fruit drinks down here, and cas is the official fruit of Costa Rica. It's natural, just the fruit, water, and sugar."

Dana had never heard of the cas fruit. She looked at Courtney and they both shrugged at almost the same time, so they ordered the same fruit drink.

"When in Rome," Dana said.

The food was delicious and the cas fruit juice was marvelous. Dana thought it tasted like grapefruit, but Courtney thought it tasted more like a lemon, but not as sour. Regardless, they both thought it was a real treat.

"We're mere minutes away from your new home," Benny said as they prepared to leave.

"It's not my home according to my cousin." Dana sighed.

"You have the paperwork to prove it, regardless of what Roy Kirkpatrick thinks," Benny replied.

"Don't even think about him," Courtney said.

"You're right. Let's go check out my new place."

FOUR

It was a quick drive from the restaurant to Casa Verde. Dana's face was glued to the window, taking in her new surroundings.

They had to drive through the entire town, which was so small that it didn't take too long, but she could take it all in.

To her right, she could see the beach with its white sand and turquoise-blue waters.

"Can't wait to take a dip in there," Courtney said. Dana just nodded her head as she continued looking around. She felt like an excited puppy looking out each window and finding something new to wag its tail over.

It was a single-lane road, but suddenly the road was divided by a raised median. Large palm trees lined the median. Dana looked up at the trees. The large fonds at the crowns of the palm trees seemed to wave at her like they were welcoming her to town. The trees were wrapped with twinkling lights, and she couldn't wait to see the beautiful palm trees lit up at night. Both sides of the median were lined up with standalone shops that looked like cottages.

"How adorable," she cooed.

"That's Ark Row on Main Street," Benny said.

"Ark Row?"

"Some of those shops used to be ark boats where local fishermen lived way back when. Eventually the municipality ordered the boats brought in from the peninsula, so they sort of just dropped them there. It took some time, but someone used one of the old ark boats to open a shop, and soon others did the same. When newer shops were built, they were forced to keep the look and feel of the original ark boats, and so now the retail center of town is known as Ark Row," Benny explained.

"Well, I'm glad they did that, because it looks so quaint and just darn adorable," Dana said. She had lowered the window down even though the car AC was blasting, but she wanted to take it all in—the looks, sounds, and smells of her new town.

After a few minutes, they had driven through the town, and Benny turned onto rough unpaved road as they began to make their way up the mountain. Dana felt like she was riding shotgun on one of the moon buggies as it made its way on the moon's surface.

It was only a few minutes until they arrived at Casa Verde. He stopped the SUV in front of a tall wall and green metal gate.

"We're here," he announced.

Dana looked around anxiously for a moment, then she heard the gate's motor coming to life as it slowly opened inward to reveal what was on the other side.

"It's like the gate at Jurassic Park," Courtney said, laughing.

On the other side of the gate, they could see luscious greenery, a lot of trees, and a man smiling eagerly at them.

He was in his early fifties and wore a long-sleeved blue coverall and a white wide-brim field hat. He waved wildly like one of the Clampetts at the end of *The Beverly Hillbillies*.

"He seems excited we're here," Dana said, waving back at the man.

"That's the caretaker, Ramón Villalobos," Benny said.

She had been told about Ramón and his wife, Carmen. They were *campesinos*, as they were referred to in Costa Rica—hard-working people that toiled the land as farmers, gardeners, caretakers, and just about any outdoor labor job that needed to be done.

Ramón's family had worked the lands around Mariposa Beach for generations.

Dana wasn't sure she could get used to having a live-in caretaker. Back in San Francisco, she had a cleaning service that would drop by every two weeks to clean her house, but a full-time arrangement, with them living on the property, made her feel awkward.

"He comes with the land," Benny had joked.

"Please don't put it that way, makes me feel all sorts of wrong inside," Dana had replied.

It wasn't just that having Ramón working and living on the property that made her wince, but she would live there by herself. So there was that added concern for her.

She wished she could run a background check, but then she would remind herself, *You're not in the States anymore, girl.*

Benny had reassured her that Ramón was a "salt of the earth" type of person who had been very loyal to her uncle Blake, who had hired him over twenty years ago and had become his trusted man Friday. Blake even built him a nice, modest home on the property.

"It would be a mistake to let someone like Ramón go," Benny had told Dana during one of their video calls a few months back.

"He's honest, hardworking, and he's always there taking care of the property, keeping it secure. There is a lot of value to that in Costa Rica. His wife Carmen is a wonderful woman; she cleaned the house and cooked for your uncle. Just you wait, she's an amazing cook," Benny had explained.

Ramón and his family lived in a bungalow-like home behind the property.

Benny explained that he kept the house and land well maintained and protected from thieves and squatters that might have pounced once word got out that Dana's Uncle Blake had become ill and had gone back to the States for medical care.

"Your uncle was adamant that Ramón received his full salary and Christmas bonus for the entire two years he was away and too sick to travel back to Costa Rica," Benny had told Dana.

It had been one of the first pieces of advice Benny had given to Dana when they first spoke about the property she was inheriting, and that was to keep Ramón and Carmen on salary and in their home so he would continue to watch and take care of the property.

Benny had explained that it was not uncommon for heirs to have properties stolen from under them by crooked lawyers and greedy developers.

Knowing that Ramón and his family lived on the property provided the needed normalcy to keep the shysters and burglars away.

"Well, I'm not too keen to toss them out of their home, and I want to honor my uncle's wishes," Dana had told Benny back then.

"I'm glad you feel that way, because that hasn't stopped other families from evicting campesino families from properties they've inherited," Benny had explained.

"Well, I'm willing to give it a shot," she responded.

Dana shook off those memories to bring herself back to reality as Benny slowly drove up through the gate and up a narrow gravel driveway.

Dana and Courtney looked around in awe; the property was brimming with trees and other lush vegetation. She had seen photographs of the property and even a video tour that Benny had recorded for her, but that didn't give the property's natural beauty its due justice.

"Wow, it's like a jungle out there," Courtney said, looking around.

"That *is* the jungle out there," Benny replied, smiling.

The driveway, from the front gate to the house, was about fifty feet.

Benny pulled up to a carport in front of the house.

Dana saw a red Willys Jeep parked in the carport, waiting for her.

It was her uncle's pride and joy, an updated and rebuilt 1948 Willys Jeep that had been decommissioned after decades of service in the U.S. Army.

The Willys looked brand new, all shiny and clean.

"That's your car?" Courtney asked. "It looks like those jeeps from *MASH*," she continued, referring to the iconic television series.

"Yeah, isn't that cool? And it looks brand new," Dana said.

"It's mostly been parked for the last two years. Looks like Ramón has taken good care of it, and I'm sure he put in an extra effort to make it shine for you," Benny said as he parked the truck and turned off the ignition.

They climbed out of the Land Cruiser and looked around. It was so green, so luscious, and so peaceful.

"That's your house!" Courtney squealed.

Dana nodded and quickly wiped a single tear from her eye.

"Dusty," Dana said, smiling.

Courtney hugged Dana as they heard footsteps scraping on the gravel. They turned and saw Ramón making his way up the driveway.

"Hola," he said cheerfully.

Benny made the introductions.

Ramón didn't speak English, so Dana and Benny spoke to him in Spanish, while Courtney, who didn't speak the language, looked around the property, kicking gravel.

"He seems sweet," Dana said to Courtney after a few minutes of chatting out in front of the house.

Dana looked up at the house and was surprised how well it looked from the outside. She breathed out nervously.

"Are you ready to go inside?" Courtney asked.

"Ready," Dana said. She looped her arm around Courtney's and they skipped forward on the gravel road like Dorothy and the Scarecrow as they broke out singing the chorus from "We're off to see the Wizard." They sang that a couple times, then they both stopped and laughed out loud.

Benny and Ramón looked at each other and shrugged with smiles on their faces.

The house sat back on a slope and was surrounded by many trees: palms, bananas, citrus fruits like oranges and lemons, and other kinds that Dana didn't recognize. The trees and vegetation were well trimmed and kept, and she began to realize that Ramón was a godsend. The house would have long been overgrown by the wild vegetation after two years, if not outright stolen by some nefarious title pirate.

Dana looked up at the wraparound front porch overhead. There was a door next to the carport. The main door to the house was up some steps to the right of the carport.

"That's your main door," Benny said, pointing towards the steps. "That door by the carport leads to a set of stairs up to the main house, it's like the mudroom concept back in the States. There is also a laundry room and a maid's room back there," Benny said, pointing at the area behind the carport.

"Maid's room?" Dana asked.

"That usually throws off Americans. It's typical in Costa Rican construction to include a maid's quarters, and not just for the rich; just about every home in Costa Rica middle-class on up has a maid's room with its own bathroom inside the main house. Usually built out back, so it's separate for privacy, like a mother-in-law suite you see back in the States sometimes. Room and board is part of the deal," Benny explained.

"Well, la-di-da, you told me your uncle's name was Blake. I didn't realize it was Blake Carrington," Courtney said, giggling.

"Ha ha. Funny, but, I'm not having a live-in maid," Dana said, sounding defensive.

"You don't have to if you don't want that. Carmen can clean your home, and you can use the maid's room for storage or another guest room or an office—whatever you want, it's your house," Benny said.

"Okay, I'm dying to walk inside," Dana said, changing the subject. She went up the short flight of front steps that led up to the door with the house keys in her hand.

She opened the door slowly. She half-expected some wild animal to come rushing out, but nothing happened.

Courtney was right behind her. "After you," Dana said to her.

"I wouldn't dare! The first person to go inside is you, my dear." She waved her arms towards the inside and did a mock bow, then she gave Dana a slight tap on her back that served as a friendly shove forward.

Dana smiled and stepped inside.

FIVE

My place, she thought as she looked around. She seemed frozen in the entryway for a moment as she stood there, taking it in.

She had been worried that, after two years of the house being empty, it would have been in sorry shape. For all she knew, the pictures she had seen were taken a while ago.

She came ready to roll up her sleeves and put in some elbow grease to fix up the place, but it was perfect.

"Wow, this is beyond move-in ready," Courtney said.

"It looks like it's been professionally staged," Dana said.

That's when Dana realized how right Benny had been about Ramón and his wife Carmen. How much hard work they had put into taking care of her uncle's landscaping, his beloved Jeep, and the house, inside and out.

For a moment, she expected her uncle to come shuffling down the hallway in his Hang Ten white shirt and well-worn flip-flops.

Dana continued to look around her new home. Although it was humid and sticky outside, thanks to the abundant amount of windows and ceiling fans, there a refreshing ocean breeze flowing through the house.

Ramón had been preparing for her arrival by airing it out. The house smelled of lemon from the cleaning supplies, courtesy of Carmen, and the smell of salt in the air was courtesy of the Pacific.

The front windows of the house offered a breathtaking view of the water, which was just a few minutes away on foot. The other windows looked out towards lush greenery of the jungle behind the property.

The beauty was overwhelming.

"It looked nice in the photographs you sent me, but...this is just stunning," Dana said, alternating looking out towards the beach and the forest.

They went upstairs, and Courtney slid the porch screen door to the side and stepped onto an ample deck overlooking the beach and the property below.

"Oh, my, Dana, come on out here, this is amazing!" she said.

The deck had a six-piece wicker patio set consisting of a middle and side sofa, two chairs, an ottoman, and a table.

"I'll just live out here," Dana said.

"Forget what I said before about moving down here. Now I'm jealous," Courtney said.

Benny joined them on the patio. He put his hands on the railing and he took in the view.

"That's Mariposa Beach down there with the safe and tranquil waters to swim in. It's a lovely community. You saw Ark Row on the drive over with its shops, and there are a few decent places to eat in town, like Soda Linda," Benny said, waving his arms from above.

"How far away is it to walk to town from here?" Courtney asked.

"Not even five minutes. You have direct access to a footpath from the side of the property that takes you down to the town and the beach. I'll show you later," he said.

He turned to his right and pointed out towards the jungle and said, "Over there, you have the Pancha Sabhai Institute, an ashram and retreat for yogis that is world famous; off to the right is a lovely bed-and-breakfast; and a couple miles from there is the Tranquil Bay Resort, that's not as quaint," Benny said, sounding ominous. "It's a luxurious five-star hotel on par with the Ritz or the Four Seasons," Benny said.

"That's a bold statement, my friend," Courtney said.

"Oh, they went all out on it. Rooms start at five hundred dollars a night. The owner of the resort loves to tell everyone that he 'spared no expense,' like the old man from Jurassic Park," Benny explained.

"Wasn't that movie filmed in Costa Rica?" Dana asked innocently.

Benny turned to look at Dana and Courtney and sighed. He said, "It was supposed to take place in Costa Rica, but it was not filmed here. What you saw on the movie screen was actually Hawaii, not Costa Rica, and don't get me started on how a brilliant filmmaker like Steven Spielberg shot that scene with Newman from *Seinfeld* supposedly in San José, sitting at a rinky-dink taco stand on the beach with chickens running around in the background...In. San. José," Benny said, halting after each word to make his point. "Can you believe that? Maybe out here, sure, but in the city? The chickens would be hit by a bus or they would die from carbon monoxide poisoning from all the traffic, and the only way to see the ocean from San José is to get in your car and drive for a few hours."

"Okay, we won't get you started," Dana said, with a thin smile on her lips.

"Sorry. It is a great movie, even with such glaring discrepancies," Benny said, clearing his throat, looking embarrassed about his rant.

"Sore subject," Courtney said with a smile.

"What else is out there?" Dana asked, changing the subject.

"Between the town, your house, and resort, there are a couple smaller, mom-and-pop type hotels and restaurants, much to the annoyance of Gustavo Barca, the Tranquil Bay owner, who would love nothing more than to buy all the land from his resort down to the beach—including yours, Dana," Benny said.

"Is that the jerk that made me an offer to buy this place?"

"That's Gustavo Barca, he's from Venezuela originally. He came from a well-off family and made a fortune in construction. Supposedly, he ran afoul of president Hugo Chavez himself, so he went on a self-imposed exile in Miami then Panama before settling in Costa Rica ten years ago, where he then went on a real estate and business buying spree and began to build his dream project, Tranquil Bay Resort," Benny said.

"Impressive," Courtney said.

"Ruthless," Benny countered. "I thought the worldwide real estate meltdown would wipe him out, but like most cockroaches, he'll survive through anything, even a nuke," he added.

"The man behind Tranquil Bay Resort sounds anything but tranquil," Dana said.

Benny laughed. "I never thought of that, but yes, very true, and unfortunately he still wants your land, bad, but we'll talk about that tomorrow or the next day. Let's not spoil your home christening with business matters just yet."

Ramón and Carmen joined the rest of the group in finishing up the tour of the house.

Dana marveled that even the kitchen had a window with a stunning view of the mountain.

There was a kitchen island with three stools that, to Dana, seemed functional, with its adjustable shelves, a knife block, a silverware tray, an organizer, towel bars, and spice racks. She remembered that Uncle Blake had been quite the cook.

To the right of the kitchen was the dining room.

A few steps from the kitchen was a comfy-looking living area furnished with a large couch, chairs, and windows that overlooked the ocean, which appeared to be held in the air from the treetops of the jungle.

Dana noticed a corridor leading towards an open archway.

"That was your uncle's nook," Benny said, having noticed Dana looking in that direction.

Dana walked towards it, feeling like she was intruding into her dead uncle's nook, but she was curious about what was back there—a man cave, a room full of surfboards? She walked down a narrow corridor and through the archway which led into a small room that stopped her cold.

"Oh, wow," Dana said. Courtney stuck her head inside to take a look.

"I knew Uncle Blake was a voracious reader, but wow," Dana said, stepping into a beautiful custom-built reading room.

It only measured around six hundred square feet, but bookshelves from the floor to the ceiling surrounded the entire room. Dana quickly counted nine rows of shelving. Dark woods. Beautifully crafted. Dana touched the edge of the shelf.

"Your uncle had that custom-made from exotic Costa Rican woods like cocobolo," Benny said.

The shelves were jam-packed with books—thousands of books, mostly paperbacks but also hardcovers.

There was a wooden ladder that flanked the entire length of the shelf. It hooked from a metal bar attached to the ceiling which allowed it to move sideways.

In the middle of the reading room sat a weatherworn and very comfortable-looking leather lounge chair and an ottoman. There was a small wooden desk flush against the wall.

"Perfect for writing," Dana said, mostly to herself.

Dana looked at the books and she smiled, remembering how much her uncle liked adventure, detective, and western novels as she saw books by Rex Stout, Clive Cussler, Zane Grey, Sue Grafton, Dashiell Hammett, Agatha Christie, John Sanford, and Dennis Lehane.

"Looks like a library," Courtney said, staring all around.

They eventually made their way upstairs to the master bedroom, which was roomy but not too ostentatious. Dana liked it.

It had a comfy-looking king-size bed that made her a little sad, thinking it was too much bed for a single girl. But her mind quickly glossed over that as she realized she had direct access to that gorgeous second-story patio from her master bedroom. The bathroom was nice, with a shower and bathtub and two sinks.

Uncle Blake didn't design this house with a single person in mind, Dana thought.

There was a guest room down the hall from the master bedroom, nicely furnished with a double bed, a nightstand, and a small sofa. The guest room had its own bathroom.

"Nice touch," Courtney said, eyeing what would be her own bathroom during her stay.

Eventually, they made their way back down to the bottom floor and down a few steps to the mudroom that paralleled the carport outside.

It was the utilitarian space of the home that housed the laundry room, storage area, and the maid's room with its own full bathroom. *Not sure what I'll do with that room,* Dana thought, looking at the space.

A back door led out to a clothesline area, and a gate from there led outside to the garden area.

There was another door at the bottom of the steps—that was the door Dana had seen when she first arrived. It led to the open carport outside.

After the tour, Dana and Courtney collapsed on the sofa on the patio. They had been touring the place and chatting for a couple hours. Benny realized he hadn't offered to take them grocery shopping, so he invited them to dinner in town, but they were too tired.

"I didn't think Costa Rica was as far as it is," Courtney said.

"We're about three thousand miles from San Francisco, girl," Dana replied.

"No wonder I'm dead tired."

It was seven p.m., and it was pitch-dark outside.

Dana and Courtney agreed to have Benny pick them up at nine a.m. for breakfast in town, and he would show them around more.

"I can't thank you enough, Benny," Dana said.

"No worries, my pleasure. And we need to talk business before I head back to San José in three days."

"Sure, and thank you."

"You're a real sweetheart, Benny, thank you for carting us around and putting up with our stuff," Courtney said, grinning.

Benny smiled and again said, "No problem."

"All right, I'll see you in the morning," he said as he got up from the chair.

Dana began to get up, but he stopped her.

"Get your rest, enjoy your first night at your new home. I know my way out."

"Señor," they heard from outside. All three of them looked over the balcony down below, and there was Ramón with a covered bowl in one hand and pitcher in the other.

Benny smiled. "I figured they weren't about to let you two go to bed without having something to eat."

Dana wanted to make sure they weren't imposing on Ramón's family's dinner.

"No, Señora, my wife makes gallo pinto for the whole week, so there is plenty of it," Ramón said, proffering the bowl and pitcher to her.

She covered the bowl with a plastic wrap that was fogged up from the hot food inside. On top of the plastic wrap was something warm wrapped in aluminum foil.

Dana took the items to the kitchen. She removed the plastic wrap, and the steam wafted in the air, smelling delicious. The bowl contained a hefty serving of gallo pinto. Benny explained that was the traditional dish of Costa Rica.

It was white rice and black beans, but that didn't really give the delicious dish its proper due. The juices from the beans mixed in perfectly with the rice.

"It's a simple recipe. You cook the rice and beans and you mix them along with some onions, cilantro, sweet pepper, salt, some water, and then you mix it all together in a pot with vegetable oil to fry it all together until it becomes gallo pinto," Benny explained to the women.

"It's a staple dish that ticos eat as a meal and as a side for breakfast, lunch, and dinner."

The aluminum foil contained six corn tortillas, and in the pitcher was a mango juice made from the fruits picked from the mango trees right on the property.

Benny turned down their offer to join them.

"I'll get something to eat at home. I'll let you enjoy your gallo pinto," he said with a smile.

"Ga-low pin-toe?" Courtney asked, butchering its pronunciation.

Dana and Benny both laughed. "Ga-yo and pinto, like the exploding car," Dana said.

"The direct translation is spotted rooster in English," Benny explained.

"Hmm, well, it looks delicious. I'm digging in," Courtney said, grabbing a spoon.

After Benny left, Dana and Courtney polished off the gallo

pinto and tortillas and most of the mango juice as they sat on the porch.

"I didn't think I was that hungry, since it wasn't that long since we ate at Soda Linda," Dana said.

"Must be the tropical heat, but I was famished."

They laughed. Then they just sat in silence for a moment, taking it all in.

"It's so quiet," Dana said after a while.

"Sounds like the rainforest ambiance noise I ask Alexa to play for me at home," Courtney said.

"Yup. Here you get the real deal."

The two friends sat on the porch for over an hour, laughing about their trip so far and how different the Guanacaste Jungle was from the concrete jungle of San Francisco.

Dana commented on how nice and helpful Benny had been and how he was going well above his lawyer duties.

"And he's cute to boot," Courtney said with a sly grin on her face.

"That's the last thing on my mind, Court."

"New start, remember?" Courtney replied. She laughed then yawned. She got up and stretched and yawned again. "I've hit the wall. I'm going to bed."

"Oh, one thing," Dana said as Courtney was heading towards her room. "Benny and Ramón warned me that if you hear a loud howling sound or rattling on the roof, not to worry, it's probably just the howler monkeys," Dana said with a grin.

"You're kidding?" Courtney asked, her eyes wide like saucers looking up at the ceiling.

"Night, night," Dana chuckled.

SIX

That there were monkeys outside was cute until they started howling like drunks stumbling out of a bar at closing.

Dana was too tired to worry about it, and she fell fast asleep until another howler monkey woke her up at six a.m. She sat straight up in bed and it took a moment to get her bearings, then she remembered, *Oh, yeah, a new bed, a new room, a new house, a new town, a new country, and a loud monkey hanging around outside.*

She lay back down, and that's when she realized there was someone in bed with her. Dana did a double take then realized it was Courtney.

It took another moment for her brain to play catch-up with her eyes, then she remembered that Courtney had crawled into her bed in the middle of the night like a child waking up from a nightmare and seeking comfort from her parents.

For Courtney, the nightmare was the loud growls from the howler monkeys, one of the loudest mammals in the world, who love to bark and grunt at night and into the early morning.

"Those monkeys are freaking me out, so sorry, but scoot

over," Courtney had said as she got into Dana's bed at around two in the morning.

Dana was too tired to argue, and she didn't mind. The bed was big enough, and she still slept way over on the right side like she had during her eight-year marriage. It was like an amputee dealing with a phantom limb, and even though she had been estranged from her now ex-husband for over a year before they began the official paperwork to divorce, she still slept on her side of the bed. She could sprawl out sideways and in the shape of a cross if she wanted. But nope, she still tucked on over to her side of the bed and stayed there.

Dana was debating about just getting up, since it seemed to be a beautiful morning outside, when another loud howl woke up Courtney, who sprung out of bed like it was on fire.

Dana watched her, laughing as she stood there for a moment.

"I never thought I could come to hate a monkey, but good gravy, I felt like Olivia de Havilland in the *Snake Pit* insane asylum," Courtney said, yawning.

As Dana was getting ready for the day, she heard the buzzer from the front gate go off.

She assumed it was Benny, arriving earlier than planned for breakfast, so she opened the gate without using the intercom.

She stepped out onto her patio and saw a small gray SUV driving up the gravel driveway. Off in the distance, she saw Ramón hacking at vegetation with a machete. *Already hard at work*, Dana thought as she turned her attention back at the approaching vehicle that was not Benny's Land Cruiser, the only vehicle in town she would recognize.

A sporty Audi Q2 pulled up to the front of the house and parked. A blonde woman decked out in Lululemon gear and wearing Warby sunglasses got out of the car and looked up to the porch and waved at Dana.

Dana waved back, not having a clue who this person was. *Maybe she's lost and thinks this is the yoga resort up the road,* Dana thought as the woman shouted up, "You must be Dana Kirkpatrick."

"I'm sorry, who are you?"

"I'm Felicia Banks with Sunshine Realty and Property Management. We exchanged a couple emails last month."

Oh, great, Dana thought, *I just buzzed in a salesperson onto the property.*

"I'll be right down," Dana said.

It took a few minutes for her to throw on her Golden State Warriors blue and gold T-shirt and a pair of gray sweatpants and make her way down from her bedroom to the front door.

Felicia Banks was looking at the property like real estate agents do. Dana noticed she was a petite blonde in her late twenties, an American, too.

"Hello there," Dana said, walking down the front steps to greet her.

"So nice to meet you finally," Banks said, sales smile on, hand out for what Dana was sure would be one of those firm, alpha-type handshakes.

Dana shook Bank's hand and yes, there it was, alpha, firm, three pumps, and a tap on her arm with her free hand, direct eye contact during the handshake. Big, toothy smile. Dana felt awkward.

"So what's up?" she asked Felicia.

"Sorry, I would have called, but I don't have your phone number. But I have a yoga class nearby, so I thought I would drop by to introduce myself," she said.

From her accent, Dana pegged the pretty realtor to be from New England.

"You're American?" Dana asked.

She nodded her head. "From Boston, originally."

Dana smiled, *Nailed it.*

"I moved out to Costa Rica five years ago, love it down here."

They chitchatted for a minute, but for Dana, Felicia was way too salesy. She was also way too perky so early in the morning. And then it dawned on Dana that she was fresh to show up that early uninvited.

Dana didn't know if this was a friendly visit, but she had Felicia pegged as all business. Making things worse, Dana hadn't had her much-needed morning coffee because she didn't have any in the house, and her body was punishing such an egregious oversight with a painful caffeine-deprived headache.

Dana had had enough. "I'm afraid I have little time this morning, my friend and I are expecting my lawyer to go over some paperwork and then we're going out to breakfast," Dana said.

"Oh, I won't be long. I know Benny well. *Very well,*" she said with a reminiscent grin.

Okay, ew. Dana thought over the insinuation. It angered her, then she stopped herself from going there.

"Yes, he's my attorney," is all Dana could say in reply.

"As I mentioned in my email, this is a very hot property you have here..." *There we go,* Dana thought as Felicia droned on, "It's such a lovely home in a very desirable part of town that would fetch a nice sum for you if you sell or keep it and rent it out. Short-term rentals are like a license to print money," Felicia said.

"I'm not interested in selling or dealing with the headaches of being a landlord," Dana said.

"Oh, I would take care of all that for you. The listing, collecting the money, home cleaning, dealing with the renters, I deal with it all, you just sit back in San Francisco and collect the money."

"I appreciate you coming out here and all, and I'm sorry I didn't have time to email you back, but I'm not going back to San Francisco, I'm moving into the house. I'm staying down here, full time," Dana said.

Felicia's face and body language went from friendly to mean girl in about two-and-a-half seconds.

"Oh. Well, that's too bad," Felicia said. Dana looked at her cross.

"Well, most expats don't last the year, so when you're ready to go back home, call me," Banks said, handing Dana her business card. *How rude,* Dana thought, but she was too annoyed and caffeine deprived to say anything, so she nodded and accepted the business card as Felicia gave her a dismissive toodle-oo wave, then turned and jumped back into her Audi.

She peeled out, kicking gravel as Dana stood there eating dust.

"What a piece of work," she said out loud to herself.

"Everything okay, Doña Dana?" Ramón asked in Spanish as he walked towards her. He was wearing his coveralls and had a machete dangling from his belt.

"Yes, she's just a realtor," Dana said, switching to Spanish.

"I know her. She was also after Don Blake to sell, and after he got sick, she would always try to get information from me about the property so she could sell or rent it," Ramón said. He could not hide his dislike for Felicia Banks, and Dana was feeling the same way.

Just at that moment, Carmen came up to her with a white thermal coffee server and two empty cups.

"Do you drink coffee?" she asked with a smile.

"Carmen, I love you."

Back inside the house, Dana poured herself a cup of coffee and splashed it with warm milk that Carmen had given her. She was just about to take a sip when Courtney walked in.

"Yes! Is that coffee? Gimme!" Courtney said all at once as she grabbed the other cup and greedily filled it. She took a deep breath of it and smiled. "Mmm, how did you score the good stuff?" she asked.

"From Carmen. She and Ramón are just sweethearts."

"Sugar?" Courtney asked.

"They offered, but I said no. I forgot you like sugar with your coffee. Sorry," Dana said.

"It's okay, this will do, but we have to hit the grocery store," she said. Courtney took a sip of coffee and asked, "So, who was the Lululemon Barbie out there?"

"A realtor. She's been after this house for years."

"You tell her that's not happening?"

"I did."

"I got that feeling from the way she peeled on out of here," Courtney said, laughing.

"Well, she showed up unannounced before eight a.m. and before I had coffee. It could have gotten a lot uglier than that."

"Question for you. I heard Ramón calling you Donna Dana. And he called Benny Don Benny. What's up with that?"

"It's old school formality. It's like saying mister or madam. And remember in *The Godfather*? Don Corleone. It's a sign of respect that's very common in Latin America," Dana explained.

"Ah, I was wondering about that."

"And there's a tilde over the N, so it's Doña, not Donna for females," Dana said, laughing.

"Okay, Doña Dana." She bobbed a curtsy to her.

They were just finishing their coffee when the front door buzzer went off again, and this time Dana pressed the intercom button.

"Yes," she said, holding the button down and speaking into it. She released the button and a man's voice crackled over the radio.

"Good morning, it's Benny."

"Come on in," Dana said, pressing the button to open the gate.

"Come on in," Courtney repeated teasingly in a sexy voice.

"Zip it, you."

SEVEN

Dana, Benny, and Courtney made their way down the footpath towards town.

On their way, Benny stopped and pointed at several black howler monkeys high on a tree. Dana looked up at them. They were big and moved slowly to gawk back at them. Some of them hung from branches from their long tails. They began to grunt and howl loudly.

"So you're the buggers that kept me awake most of the night," Courtney said, glaring at her newly minted enemies of sleep.

"Oh, but they're so cute," Dana said.

"Yes, God made them cute so we don't wring their necks," Courtney replied.

The smallest monkey of the group flung forward on a branch as if to inspect the three weird-looking humans looking back at them. The sudden movement startled Dana and Courtney, and the monkey seemed to enjoy that very much, as it started hooting and howling and shaking from the edge of the tree's branch.

"Oh, that's him, the little guy is the loudest one!" Courtney said.

The little creature seemed to smile and darted back up the tree to join the others.

"I think that one there has a Napoleon complex," Dana said.

"Yeah, keep it up, Napoleon, and I will exile you to the island of Elba too," Courtney yelled up at the tree as they laughed and continued on their way into town.

As they reached the edge of town, they saw a large iguana that was lying out on a rock to catch a blast of the morning sun.

"He looks like Godzilla," Courtney said as she dug out her iPhone and took a picture.

"Remind me to bring back a banana. Iguanas love to munch on fruit," Benny said.

"Really? I thought they ate bugs, like a frog," Dana said.

"Iguanas are not meat eaters, they're herbivorous. They mostly eat plants. But they like fruits, as well."

"Well, I'll be, I didn't realize Godzilla over there was a vegetarian," Courtney said.

"They just look scary, but they're little sweethearts," Benny said.

They were just about to spill out onto Main Street when Dana told Benny about Felicia's visit earlier that morning.

"She's very good at her job, but she appears way too pushy, which can be good if she's working on your behalf, trying to sell or rent your property, but very annoying when you're on the other side of that transaction," Benny explained. "And when she's zeroed in onto something, hide your feet, because she'll step all over your toes to get what she wants."

"She mentioned that she knew you well," Dana said.

"It's a small community here. We all know each other well."

"She said she knew you *very* well, with a hard emphasis on the very," Dana said. She smiled at watching him blush.

"Oh, that...We dated a few times. But that was well over a year ago. It didn't work out."

"Sorry, I didn't mean to pry," Dana said, feeling guilty about snooping into his personal life.

"I'm not sorry, so spill the beans, Benny. What happened there? Who ended it?" Courtney chimed in.

"Courtney!" Dana said.

"What? We're all adults," Courtney replied.

Benny laughed and said, "It's okay. I ended it, but we really didn't have a big relationship. We dated for about a month. I didn't see it blossoming into anything serious, and with me spending most of my time in San José, it just made little sense to continue dating. She agreed. So nothing too juicy about it, sorry."

The trio made their way down the footpath until they spilled out to an unpaved road which connected to the town's Main Street, which was an inside joke with the locals since it was the only street through town.

"Only Street," Benny said, chuckling. He explained that was the name many of the locals used to mock the Ark Row merchants' attempt to give tourists a Main Street USA vibe to Mariposa Beach's only thoroughfare.

They walked to the Qué Vista Restaurant. Qué Vista was Spanish for *what a view*, and the name was spot-on. The restaurant was on the beach with its tables on a wooden deck right on the sand with a direct view of the water.

They enjoyed their breakfast and drank more coffee with the sounds of the waves crashing onto the shore. Afterwards, Benny said, "I hate to switch gears from such a lovely morning, but we need to talk about some legal matters."

"The dreaded L-word," Dana said jokingly.

"There have been updates we need to discuss, so why don't

we walk back to Casa Verde? I have some documents in my truck, and we'll sit down and have a chat."

"Okay, okay," Dana said, smiling.

The three of them were walking down Main Street by Ark Row as they were heading back to the footpath when a passing car slammed on the brakes right as it drove past them.

The car's sudden stop was jarring, so all three of them were looking at the darkly tinted windows of the vehicle as it began to back up towards them.

"Dana," a man's voice called out from inside the car. Hearing her name startled her, since she had only met a few people in the day since she arrived.

Dana looked down into the passenger window which was being rolled down. She was wondering who was inside, then, when she saw who it was, she felt like she would deposit her breakfast right there on Main Street.

Glaring back at her was Skylar Kirkpatrick, wife of Dana's cousin, Roy Kirkpatrick, the only son of her Uncle Blake.

Roy was behind the wheel. Unlike Skylar, he seemed more sad than mad at seeing Dana. But the negative energy coming from the car was palpable for Dana as she stood up stiffly and glanced over at Courtney and Benny.

"It's my cousin and his wife."

"Hey, Dana, I heard you were coming to town," Roy said. He got out of the car and came around to where Dana was standing. Skylar stayed in the car with a scowl on her face as she checked her fingernails.

"Hi, Roy," Dana said unenthusiastically.

Roy was ten years older than Dana. He had always been plump and stocky. Even though their fathers didn't get along, she and Roy had been close as kids, despite the age difference.

But as they became adults, they began to see less and less of each other. It didn't help that he became estranged from not just his father, but the whole family, and that he had moved to another state.

She hadn't seen him in person in over ten years. Their only interactions over the years had been on Facebook, where they exchanged a few likes here and there, but even that felt awkward for Dana.

He smiled at her and he seemed embarrassed, since they were involved in a legal dispute over Casa Verde.

There was no contrition or hint of regret from his wife, Skylar. She was abrasive and nasty, and since they became entangled in a legal dispute over the Casa Verde property, Skylar had gone to Defcon 2, and Defcon 1 seemed imminent to Dana.

Dana felt weird; after not seeing Roy in person for so long, to run into him in tiny Mariposa Beach was surreal.

"What are you doing here, Roy?" Dana asked innocently. She didn't mean to come off defensive or confrontational, but Skylar jumped out of the car and charged towards her like a road-raging fool. She might as well have told Roy to get lost.

"Oh, that's rich, Dana. No, no, no! You don't get to ask him that question. We're the ones who should ask you, what are you doing here?" She stood there with both hands on her hips.

Dana sighed. It was a silly argument to get into.

"I meant nothing by it, I was just surprised to run into you guys, that's all."

"You have some nerve. That's our house you moved into..." Skylar shoved her thumb into her chest as if to drive home the point further, and then continued getting louder. "You're squatting in *our* house. It doesn't belong to you," Skylar barked as loud as the howler monkeys.

Roy looked down at the ground, looking for dirt to kick in an aw-shucks way.

Skylar had always run roughshod over him.

Benny and Courtney both stepped forward towards Dana so they were standing side-by-side in protective mode.

"I'm not getting into that with you again, Skylar. Uncle Blake left me that property. I'm sorry, but that was his decision. It was in black and white in his will," Dana reminded her.

"Yeah, well, it's not over, squatter, not by a long shot."

"It's not fair, Dana, he was my father," Roy said, sounding more hurt than angry.

"Roy—" Dana tried to talk to her cousin, but Skylar interrupted.

"See you in court, squatter," she said.

"Okay, that's enough, we *will* see you in court," Benny interjected.

"Sorry, Dana, but I was his only son. It's not right," Roy said, before looking back at the ground looking for that dirt to kick.

"Don't apologize to her, dummy!" Skylar screeched. "Come on, Roy, lets go, *now*." She got back into the car, slamming the door shut so hard that Dana expected it to fall off its hinges.

Roy was making his way back around the car to the driver's side, but he must have been too slow for Skylar, who yelled out, "Can you move any slower? Come on, *today*. I swear you move slower than a sloth. It's like one hundred degrees out here, I need the AC turned on *now*!"

Roy started the car, and as he drove away, Dana could still hear Skylar berating him. "I swear, you're as dumb as a bag of hair." That was the last thing she heard her say before the car drove off.

"Don't you just love family reunions?" Dana asked, tears welling in her eyes.

"Wow. She's a peach, isn't she?" Courtney replied. During the whole confrontation, she stood there dumbfounded, and in a rare instance for her, speechless.

Dana turned to Benny. "She said she would see me in court.

I guess that's what we were going to discuss when we got back to Casa Verde?"

Benny blushed and cleared his throat. "Yes, that's the legal matter that I have been meaning to talk to you about. I didn't know they were in town. I would have discussed this with you right away if I knew that. I'm really sorry about that."

"It's okay. I'll find out soon enough what's going on."

Dana sighed as she looked up towards the Ark Row shops, where a small crowd of onlookers had gathered to see what was going on with the commotion.

Dana could feel their judging eyes upon her after witnessing her family dysfunction on full display on Main Street.

Way to make a great first impression in front of your new neighbors, Dana thought, feeling embarrassed.

"Well, Benny, let's get back home so you can tell me what all that was about."

EIGHT

Back at Casa Verde, Dana, Benny, and Courtney sat on stools around the kitchen's center island. It had been over twenty minutes after her confrontation with Skylar and Roy, but it felt like twenty seconds to her.

Benny looked at her with sympathetic eyes and a thin smile.

"Roy is contesting the will," he said.

"I know, but that was all taken care of in San Francisco. It took months, but the judge ruled in my favor," Dana said.

"Yes, but that was in the States. Roy's hired an attorney in Costa Rica and he's contesting the will here," Benny explained.

"He can do that?" Courtney asked.

"Yes. We're dealing with two separate jurisdictions, so even though the will was written in California and your uncle was still a U.S. citizen, the property is on Costa Rican soil. I was hoping the Costa Rican court would squash it because of the San Francisco ruling, but the judge agreed that since the property is in this country and that your uncle had been a legal resident of Costa Rica for over twenty years, that it was their right to also contest the will here," Benny explained.

Dana took in the information quietly. The last thing she

wanted to do was get immersed in yet another legal dispute about Casa Verde. But she had that Kirkpatrick stubbornness in her.

"I beat Roy in California, I can beat him here," she said, trying to sound resolute. As soon as she said that, she began to feel less confident about it. "Right?" she asked Benny.

Benny smiled. "Roy's American lawyers tried to poke holes into your uncle's will, but thankfully for you and in honor of your uncle's final wishes, the will was excellently drafted. It's as ironclad as they come. The fact that it was upheld and the courts in California ruled in your favor will help us here in the long run. So I like our chances, but one can never be one hundred percent certain when it comes to the legal system," Benny said.

"How long will all this take?" Dana asked.

"Like all legal processes, it's slow."

Dana sighed loudly.

"I'm curious," Benny said, tapping his fingers on the countertop, "how can Roy afford all these legal fees? I looked at the legal documents filed in the California courts, and they were in a financial pickle when they contested the will. Neither him nor Skylar had high-paying jobs. Yet, they had decent lawyers up there, and they just hired one of the best lawyers in Costa Rica to handle their case here."

"Oh, great," Dana said.

"Sorry, didn't mean to upset you. I know this is coming out of the blue. I received notice from their attorney yesterday, so I don't have too much information yet."

"I don't know how Roy and Skylar can afford all these lawyers. He's always jumped from one business venture to the next, which have all ended up in failure. She's worked as a dental assistant and a receptionist, not a lot of money for high-powered lawyers in those jobs."

"Didn't Roy get some money from your uncle?" Courtney asked.

"Roy inherited ten thousand dollars in cash. Dana was the main beneficiary, getting this property, the Jeep, and the publishing rights to Blake's surfing and travel books, which are nice little earners," Benny replied.

Dana fidgeted on the stool. She had wrestled with the guilty feelings of being named as the main beneficiary to her uncle's estate, and she understood why Roy was upset. She might have even come to some sharing agreement with Roy, but Skylar went for the jugular from the start and once the lawyers got involved, it was all or nothing for one of them, and she had won fair and square in California. And now Roy and Skylar wanted to keep fighting by moving the legal matters to Costa Rica in another attempt to toss out her uncle's final will and testament because Roy and Skylar didn't like what was in it.

"Do they even want to move here?" Courtney asked.

"No way. I know Skylar hates it down here. She's more L.A. than Mariposa Beach, Costa Rica," Dana replied.

"They probably want Casa Verde so they can sell it. This property is worth a nice chunk of change. That is why Felicia was all over you this morning. Trying to get first crack at it," Benny said.

"Skylar just wants to flip it," Dana said.

"That will also help your case. You have moved in, they just want to sell it and take the cash out of Costa Rica and back to the States," Benny said.

"But the fact that they're here, I wouldn't put it past her to lie and say she wants to live here and how I'm just a squatter," Dana said.

"They can say anything they want. It's what's in your uncle's will that matters. It will be my job to prove that their claims are hogwash," Benny said, flashing a reassuring smile to Dana.

That night, Dana went to bed certain she would toss and turn all night, but she fell fast asleep until strange pitter-patter sounds coming from the roof awoke her. She grabbed her mobile phone, and it was one in the morning and the racket up on the roof was getting louder. She went for the bedroom light when she heard Courtney scurrying down the hallway towards her room. She flicked the lights on as Courtney came in without knocking and jumped into bed with Dana.

"I think Napoleon is trying to break in," Courtney said, eyes darting up towards the ceiling, expecting to see the howler monkeys come crashing through it.

"Could also be raccoons. Ramón said they have a lot of them here," Dana said.

Ramón had warned her about mapaches, the Spanish word for raccoons, that were always hanging around and up to no good in the dead of night. He was constantly shoring up his chicken coop to keep the mapaches and other carnivorous predators out.

"Raccoons, howling monkeys. It's like the Wild Animal Kingdom up there," Courtney said, her eyes glued to the ceiling.

"Well, I doubt it can get in, whatever it is."

"Oh, that's reassuring. How can you be so calm?" Courtney said, her voice almost a whisper.

"Why are you whispering?" Dana asked in a mock whisper.

Suddenly they heard the noise again. Something was definitely walking up on the roof.

That's when Dana saw, from the corner of her eye, a small shadow drop down onto the patio's railing from above.

Courtney saw it too and yelped.

"Jeez, Court, you're going to give me a heart attack. It's probably a raccoon," Dana said, grabbing her flashlight.

"Some wild animal is out there lurking in the shadows, and I'm giving you the heart attack?" Courtney asked.

Dana smiled, and she stepped forward towards the closed glass patio door while Courtney stepped backward, away from the bedroom.

Dana glanced over at Courtney and laughed upon seeing her by the door.

"You're such a chicken," Dana said, turning on her flashlight and pointing it outside.

She shone the flashlight from the glass patio door, which made it difficult to see anything through the glass, but she saw two bright yellow eyes staring back at her.

"Something is out there, all right," Dana said.

"Just let it be, hopefully it will go away," Courtney said. She had now backed out completely from the master bedroom and was standing out in the hallway, her arms crossed on her chest.

Intrigued, Dana flipped the switch to the lights of the patio, and sitting on the edge of the patio's balcony sat a cat, staring at her.

The cat didn't even flinch when the lights to the patio flooded out the darkness.

"It's just a cat," Dana said, looking back towards Courtney, who had taken a few steps forward and re-entered the master bedroom. "It's cute," Dana said.

Courtney saddled up next to her.

Dana was in a stare down standoff with the kitty, but the cat wouldn't budge. It sat there looking at her, then began to meow.

Dana unlocked the patio door.

"Are you nuts? Don't go out there," Courtney pleaded.

"It's just a cat," Dana said.

"It's probably a feral cat that won't let you get near it."

"It's too friendly, too curious, to be feral. A feral cat won't sit there meowing at humans," Dana said.

"Okay, then it's a stray cat that might be infested with fleas and who knows what other jungle kung-fu juju it might have," Courtney said.

Dana ignored her and opened the patio door and slowly stepped outside. She put her flashlight down so as not to scare the intruder.

The cat watched her closely as she got closer and slowly extended her hand to the cat, saying, "Hello, kitty."

The cat was as white as the sand out on the beach. It had a black marking on its snout and forehead. Unique markings from the cats she had seen in the tropics.

"You are gorgeous," Dana said as she slowly walked up to it.

The cat bowed its little head as if to say *you may pet me*. So Dana did just that as the cat began to purr wildly while she scratched its little scalp and behind its right ear.

"It's for sure not feral," Dana said as she continued to scratch its head, chin, and rump as the cat arched its back and purred in bliss.

Finally, Courtney felt it was safe enough to join Dana outside on the patio.

"It is a cute cat, I'll give you that," Courtney said.

"Aren't you a little Flying Wallenda? Trapezing down from the rooftop, landing in perfect form. I will call you Wally in honor of the Flying Wallendas," Dana said, talking to the cat like he understood a word she was saying.

"Oh, don't name the cat, you'll never be able to get rid of it if you name stray animals," Courtney warned.

"Why would I want to get rid of it? Wally is adorable," Dana cooed.

"He is cute," Courtney said. "Is it a he or a she?"

"I don't know yet. I don't want to take a peek and spook it," Dana said. "I'm going to give it some water," she said, dashing off to the bathroom.

"A name, water, it will never leave now," Courtney said. She too was now scratching Wally behind the ears.

Wally drank some water, purred some more, and then did an Iggy Pop-like stage dive from the porch to the ground down below. Dana and Courtney both rushed to look down to make sure it was okay. Dana used the flashlight to see Wally strutting around by the driveway like it owned the place. Dana followed it with her flashlight as the cat crossed the driveway and disappeared into the shrubbery.

"I wonder if he'll come back," Dana said wistfully.

"Like I said, you've named it and given it water, he'll be back," Courtney said, and yawned. "I'm going back to sleep."

NINE

Wally didn't come back jumping on the roof, and Napoleon and the other howler monkeys were quieter that night, or perhaps she was getting used their loud nightly shenanigans.

Dana got up early. She realized that with all the commotion, she still hadn't made it to the grocery store, and her fridge and cupboards were pathetically empty.

The only grocery store in town opened early. Courtney was asleep, so Dana ran out to the store to pick up a few things for breakfast at home.

A few minutes later, she pulled into one of the ten parking spots in front of the Super Fresh Market which was on Main Street across from Ark Row.

It was a small grocery store with just a few aisles and limited shelf space. She had barely set foot inside where she was greeted warmly by Ernesto and Dora Castro, the owners of the market.

"We've heard so much about you," Dora said excitedly.

"You have?" Dana asked. She felt uncomfortable and befuddled. *Is the whole town talking about me?* she wondered to herself.

"It's a small community, word travels fast, you'll find out once you're all settled in," Ernesto said, smiling widely. "Especially since you're Blake's niece. We miss that old surfer. He was a great man and did a lot for the community," he added.

Dana smiled. She liked to hear all these wonderful stories about her uncle, since all she heard from her father and mother was that Blake was a beach bum who had thrown away a promising career in academia to write silly travel books and live down in the tropics. Dana was sure that if her father were still alive, he would have been beyond mortified that she was following her uncle Blake's footsteps to the tropics. Her mother disapproved, nothing new there.

She began to peruse the shelves, and she marveled at the selection of organic foods available.

"I'm impressed with your organic selection," Dana said, smiling.

Ernesto thanked her and explained that it was necessary to meet the demands of the health-conscious yogi tourists that flocked to the Nosara area beaches and its yoga retreats.

Dana felt a twinge of guilt. It was obvious this grocery store catered to the tourists and expats, not the locals, who could hardly afford to shop there.

After about twenty minutes and well stocked with groceries, Dana headed back to Casa Verde. She was making breakfast when Courtney made her way downstairs to the kitchen following the scent of freshly brewed coffee and bacon.

"I love you," Courtney said dramatically as she poured herself a cup of coffee.

They ate scrambled eggs that Dana cooked with chunks of bacon, spinach, and onions and buttered wheat toast, along with papaya and pineapple that Dana had just cut up.

"Some feast you rustled up," Courtney said.

"I can whip a mean breakfast, but that's about it."

"Well, you got me beat, I tried to boil some eggs, and I forgot about them until I got a whiff of this awful smell and I ran out to the stove and the water had evaporated and the eggs were all black and burned and nasty. The pot didn't make it."

"Didn't that happen to you twice?"

"Maybe."

They were just about finished eating when they heard loud meows coming from outside.

"That must be Wally!" Dana said, sounding excited.

"He must have smelled that bacon. It got me downstairs," Courtney said.

Dana opened the front door and Wally sauntered in like he belonged. He looked up at Dana and he rubbed his little furry head against her leg.

"Looks like he recognizes you," Courtney said.

Dana bent over and carefully picked up the cat, not knowing how it would react, but it loved it; it began to purr and meow sweetly.

"Looks like you got yourself a pet," Courtney said.

"I guess so. I've always been more of a dog person, but he's too darn cute."

"Seems friendly like a dog versus your typical aloof cat," Courtney said, checking out the friendly cat. "Oh, Wally is a boy, I just checked," Courtney said, grinning.

"Good, so the name fits."

Dana made a little plate of scrambled eggs with bacon bits for Wally, which the kitty ate while purring the whole time.

"You've broken the seal. He will never leave now," Courtney said, smiling.

After yesterday's confrontation with Roy and Skylar, Dana was feeling reclusive and didn't want to leave Casa Verde. She had to wait for Benny, who was going to bring some legal documents for her to sign, but in the meantime she had nothing to do.

It took some prodding from Courtney to get her to change her mind.

"There is no point in staying put, sulking about your cousin and his psycho wife."

"You're right. I'm not letting them bring me down."

"Atta girl!"

So Dana and Courtney spent the rest of the morning and early afternoon at the beach, trying to relax.

The water was warm and calm, with gentle waves coming in groups of twos and threes.

They lay on large beach towels on the white sand. Dana brought two of her uncle's books to read: *Surfing Costa Rica* was his classic guide to surfing, and *The Expats' Guide To Living Like a Tico*, a how-to book for foreigners dreaming of ditching their hated jobs back home to live in a tropical paradise on a budget.

Dana was engrossed in the books, and marveled at the humor and how well her uncle wrote. She felt bad that it was the first time she had read any of his stuff.

When it got too hot, they would run into the water, hopping barefoot on the sand like they were walking on hot coals. After a few refreshing minutes in the water, they would go back to the towels.

Later in the afternoon, Dana and Courtney went to the Qué Vista restaurant for lunch. She was able to meet the owner, Maria Rivera, who also seemed excited about Dana moving into town. They also met a character by the name of Mike Pavlopoulos, who was eating a chicken casado. He was a Greek-American expat that went by the name of Big Mike, which Dana found odd, being that he was a scrawny 160 pounds and was about five feet six inches tall.

Dana figured Courtney must have been surprised, because she blurted out to him, "Why do they call you Big Mike?"

Dana winced. The last thing she wanted to do was insult members of the community she was trying to join, plus she worried there was a sordid story behind the nickname.

Big Mike smiled widely. It was obvious it wasn't the first time someone had asked him why a short, skinny guy had that nickname, and that he loved to tell the story.

"I used to be a pro big wave surfer. I surfed Mavericks. Twice," Big Mike said, beaming with pride.

It impressed Dana. Mavericks was a world-known big-wave surfing competition held near Half Moon Bay, California, which was about thirty miles south of San Francisco.

Big Mike got excited when Dana told him they were from San Francisco and knew all about the fifty-foot waves of Mavericks.

After chatting about surfing and the Bay Area for a couple minutes, something dawned on Dana.

"Wait a sec, so Big Mike, like on that surf shop we saw over on Main Street?" she asked.

"That's me. I came down here in the eighties to surf, and eventually I moved down here. Opened up the surf shop almost twenty years ago," Big Mike said proudly. "I loved your uncle. I came down here for the very first time with not much more than my surfboard and a dog-eared copy of his surfing guide."

That made Dana smile wide.

He talked and looked like the stereotypical Southern California surfer.

"What part of California are you from originally?" Dana asked.

Big Mike laughed. "I'm from Lawrence, Kansas. I was born and raised a Jayhawk."

"Not a lot of big waves in Kansas, Big Mike," Courtney said teasingly.

"Well, I moved to California when I was eighteen—right after I graduated from high school," Big Mike explained.

"I had you pegged as being from Long Beach."

"Thanks," Big Mike said proudly. "Well, I have to get going back to the shop," he said, reaching for his wallet to pay for his lunch. "Make sure to stop by sometime to check it out and say hello. I'll get you two out on those waves," he said as he walked away in his white muscle shirt, bright orange longboard shorts, and ultra-green flip-flops.

"So here's where Jeff Spicoli wound up at," Courtney said with a giggle.

Dana and Courtney walked back to Casa Verde. She would meet there with Benny later that afternoon.

It surprised her that he was already at the house waiting for them.

"Hi, Benny, did I have the wrong time? I thought we were meeting at four?"

"No, I'm early. I need to tell you something urgently. I didn't want to do it over the phone, so I just drove over. Ramón let me in to wait for you."

He seemed somber and glum, which made her nervous. Did the courts somehow quickly decide against her and she had lost Casa Verde to Roy and Skylar?

"Did we lose the legal battle already?"

"No, it's not that."

"What is it? You're freaking me out," Dana said.

"Yeah, dude, me too," Courtney added.

"Sorry. You were at the beach?" Benny asked.

"Yes."

"Obviously you heard nothing...about Roy?" Benny asked, sounding concerned.

"No, what now? He's suing me for swimming in his ocean?"

"Not sure how to put this," Benny said.

"Just put it out there," Dana replied, a trace of annoyance in her voice.

"Roy is dead."

TEN

Dana felt terrible. She stepped out to the porch to gather her thoughts and process the news. Wally followed her out, meowed condolences, then plopped down by her feet.

She couldn't help but think no matter their legal squabbles, Roy was family. And even though the Kirkpatrick family was very dysfunctional, so were a lot of other families, and Roy was still her blood and now he was dead. And he died with them fighting over land.

She felt even worse that their last words and looks exchanged the previous day had been so acrimonious.

Benny and Courtney left her alone for a few minutes to process the news.

"I'm sorry," Benny said, walking up to her slowly. Courtney walked up and hugged Dana tightly.

"What happened?" Dana finally asked.

"He was murdered," Benny said.

"Murdered? How can that be?"

"Details are still up in the air," Benny said.

"When did this happen?" Dana asked.

"I was told that he was killed late last night, and they found his body about an hour ago," Benny replied.

"Oh, sheesh," Dana said, covering her mouth with her trembling hand. "A robbery gone bad?" she asked after a moment of silence.

"I know nothing about that yet," Benny said.

"So what happens now?"

"There is no police presence in Mariposa Beach, it's too small of a town. The closest police substation is in Playa Guiones, so they'll send a policeman to the scene from there. It's about a twenty-minute drive, so I'm sure he's here by now," Benny explained.

"The police force is different here than in the States," Benny said. "Unlike the city police departments in the States, towns don't have their own police force. We have a National Police Force. The cops enforce the law nationally from stations and substations all over the country. But the police do not investigate crimes. They can't even charge anyone with a crime. That falls under the auspices of the Organismo de Investigación Judicial, OIJ, the Judicial Investigation Department, which is a unit of the Supreme Court of Justice of Costa Rica. The Judicial Police has jurisdiction in the entire country and its detectives are the only ones who can actually investigate a crime and charge individuals with crimes, not the national police force. The OIJ detectives are sort of like a San Francisco Police detective and an FBI agent, rolled into one."

"So the cop coming from Guiones, he won't start investigating?" Dana asked.

"No. Their role is to come here to secure the scene and make sure no one messes with it while they wait for the OIJ to send detectives to investigate. The Guiones police force is tiny, just a few cops on dirt bikes that are part of the Tourist Police," Benny explained.

"Tourists have their own cops?" Courtney asked.

"Tourism is a two-billion-dollar business. Costa Rica was the most visited nation in the Central American region, with millions of foreign visitors coming here every year. Especially in these small beach communities that rely on ecotourism but have never had their own police force. So if something happened, the closest National Police Station was up in Nosara, so even if they sent a police car right away, it would take about thirty minutes to get here, even further for some of the other beach communities south of here. So they opened these small Tourist Police substations in the most popular beach towns like Guiones. We're still too small for our own substation, but at least there is one in Guiones, so a police officer can get down here pretty quickly," Benny explained.

"The real kick in the pants is that if you want to report a crime or file a complaint against someone, the police can't do that, only the OIJ, so the victim would have to drive to the nearest OIJ station, which is all the way up in Nicoya, to file a crime report, so obviously, very few crimes get reported, especially small stuff like pickpockets or a car break-in," Benny said.

"No wonder the crime rate is so low here, when it's not reported," Dana said, shaking her head.

"Because Roy was murdered, the case will be fast-tracked, especially him being American, so I'm sure the OIJ has already sent someone down to investigate. But Nicoya is about a two-hour car ride away, and even though they can zoom down faster with their lights flashing, the concept of pulling over for emergency vehicles is still a work in progress here," Benny said.

"That's crazy," Courtney said.

"Welcome to the tropics," Benny replied.

"Well, I can't just sit around here waiting for hours. Can you take me to the crime scene?" Dana asked.

"That's not a good idea, Dana," Benny warned as Courtney nodded her head in agreement.

But her old investigative journalism spirit had kicked in, and it was stubborn when rekindled, so ten minutes later, Benny was driving Dana and Courtney to the scene of the crime.

"They found his body in the brush off the footpath; about midway between your house and the Tranquil Bay Resort," Benny said as he drove.

"They weren't staying there, were they?" Dana asked.

"That's what I was originally coming to talk to you about. I found out they've been in Costa Rica for three months. They've been staying at the resort," Benny said.

"The super swanky one you mentioned the other night? The five-star one that starts at five hundred dollars a night?" Dana asked incredulously.

"That's the one."

"How could they possibly afford to stay there for three months?"

"It took a little digging, but I found out where all this money was coming from to pay legal fees, room and board, and more," Benny said. He stopped talking to maneuver the Land Cruiser around a huge pothole.

The pothole avoided, he continued, "Gustavo Barca is their benefactor; he's been bankrolling Roy and Skylar one hundred percent."

"The developer guy from Venezuela?" Dana asked.

"Yes. And he also owns the Tranquil Bay Resort, so it makes sense he would put them up there," Benny said.

"Why would he do that?" Courtney asked.

"He wants my property," Dana replied, staring out the window.

"That's my guess. Gustavo Barca is not known for his charity work, but for being ruthless and one-track minded when he wants something, and he wants his resort to connect to the beach via his own private-access land, so he's been buying up land like crazy, and there is the Pancha Sabhai Institute, a bed and breakfast, a private farm, and your property in his way."

"A bunch of yogi monks, a farmer, and little old me. Barca must like his odds," Dana said, sighing.

ELEVEN

Dana should have listened to Benny, who had warned her not to go down to the scene of the crime.

"I shouldn't have gone out there," she whispered to Benny and Courtney on the quiet drive back to Casa Verde.

Why did I insist? she thought to herself.

Thirty minutes earlier they had pulled up across the entrance to the footpath that led from the town up the mountainside towards the Tranquil Bay Resort. There was yellow crime scene tape hung between two palm trees that blocked access to the footpath.

If that wasn't enough deterrent, there was a police motocross bike parked diagonally in front of the tape and a bored-looking uniformed police officer leaning up against one of the palm trees, looking at his cell phone.

The police officer was young—in his late twenties. He was wearing the uniform of the Costa Rican Tourist Police: a blue baseball hat with POLICIA, Spanish for POLICE, emblazoned in bright yellow on the cap, a short-sleeved white polo shirt with a blue collar, and a couple of official-looking chest patches embroidered into the shirt. Blue cargo pants were equipped with a utility belt with a set of shiny handcuffs dangling on one side and a holster with the officer's service pistol on the other side.

Benny peered out the window and said, "That's Freddy Sanchez."

"How well do you know him?" Dana asked.

"There are only a few cops in the Playa Guiones substation who oversee all the small beach towns on the coast in the Nosara district, so you get to know most of them after a while. He's a good cop. Nice and honest," Benny said.

"When you said tourist police, I was expecting a Baywatch lifeguard type," Courtney said.

"Oh, no, these guys get a lot of flack, even from other cops in the national police force, but they're actual cops. They're not lifeguard or tour guides. They go through the same training as any police officer in Costa Rica at the National Police Academy. They face a lot of the same dangers, that is why they're armed. They're not all about giving tourists directions. They have added skills—for example, they require all tourist police officers to speak English, and they need to have a very cordial, friendly, and outgoing personality, since they are the face tourists will see when something bad has happened to them," Benny explained.

Dana and Courtney followed Benny as he approached Officer Sanchez, who looked up from his phone and pocketed it when he saw the trio coming his way.

"Sorry, Don Benny, the footpath will be closed for a couple days. You must go around the mountain."

"I know, Freddy, this is the cousin of the victim," Benny said, pointing towards Dana. He introduced them to each other.

Dana could see Officer Sanchez stiffen up. He looked at her and Courtney and offered them a funeral director smile and said in excellent English, "I'm sorry, ma'am, but I can't let anyone through, even family."

"Is the OIJ on the way?" Benny asked.

Sanchez nodded and said, "Detective Picado is coming."

Benny sighed. "We should go," Benny whispered to Dana when they heard a woman scream so loud that it made everyone jump and Officer Sanchez to put his hand on the butt of his gun.

Dana turned and saw Skylar Kirkpatrick coming towards her even more aggressively than she had done so yesterday.

"You murderer!" Skylar yelled as she got closer.

Instinctively, Benny and Courtney stepped in front of Dana in case Skylar would physically attack her.

Officer Sanchez looked at the two groups of people and he got into a defensive stand in the middle. He held his left hand out, his palm facing Skylar, and said in a commanding voice, "Stop right there, ma'am, and please do not come any closer."

Skylar continued to force Sanchez to stop her by gently putting the palm of his hand on her shoulder. "Ma'am, please stop!" he said, his voice inflicting upwards. He wasn't yelling, and the last thing he wanted to do was to arrest the widow of the murder victim, but he couldn't let her assault Dana.

"Ma'am, please stop," he said again in that commanding voice cops around the globe use.

Skylar finally snapped from her rage trance and she stopped and looked at Sanchez.

"She killed my husband," Skylar said to the police officer.

"We'll handle it, right now I need you to please step back and go back to your hotel until we call you," Sanchez said.

Skylar took two steps back and said, pointing her finger at Dana, "That's her, the woman I told you about. She killed my beloved husband. They've been feuding for years and she stole my husband's property right from under him, but he wasn't letting her get away with it, and so he was taking her to court. So she killed him so she can keep it all for herself."

Sanchez glanced over at Benny, still standing between them and Skylar with his hand out.

Dana felt a rush of anger. *How dare she?* But she bit her lip and said nothing. It made little sense to get into it with Skylar. No matter how she treated Roy and the fact that she was now referring to him as her "beloved husband" was laughable, but she had just lost Roy, so she felt she had to keep quiet and let her vent. Dana wasn't sure what she would say anyway. She and Skylar didn't get along, but the acidic tone in Skylar's voice dumbfounded her, and it shocked her that she would accuse her of killing Roy.

"Well, arrest her, she's killed my husband!" Skylar yelled at Sanchez.

"That is not true," Benny said calmly to Officer Sanchez.

"Ma'am, like I told you before, the OIJ investigators are on their way. We all need to stay calm and be patient as they have to make their way down from Nicoya, and they'll want to talk to you so you can provide them with any information you think is important," Sanchez said calmly to Skylar.

He then turned and looked at Dana and said, "They'll want to talk to you, too, ma'am, so please go back to your house and wait for the investigators to contact you."

"Her house?" Skylar seethed. "Didn't you hear what I just told you? Are you stupid or just incompetent? That is my husband's house, my house. Not hers!" Skylar shouted as a small crowd of onlookers began to gather around to check out yet another commotion she was involved in. She felt mortified.

"Get me out of here," Dana whispered to Benny as she felt her knees buckle.

Courtney grabbed Dana by the arm and the three of them walked back to the car as Skylar continued to shout at Dana, calling her a murderer and berating the police officer for not doing anything.

As Benny drove off, Dana could hear Skylar shouting obscenities for what seemed like miles on end.

TWELVE

Back at Casa Verde, Dana was a mess. She yo-yoed between grief and anger. It upset her that Skylar accused her of murder in front of her friends, her new community, and especially in front of the police.

"The nerve of that woman," Courtney said.

As upset as Dana was, she tried to see it from Skylar's perspective—as hard as that was to do.

"She just lost her husband. Murdered. People say crazy things when overwhelmed with grief. She wants someone to blame right away, and I was an easy target when she saw me there. You guys were right. I should have never gone out there," Dana said. Wally jumped on her lap, making her feel better. She wondered if he could sense she felt down.

"Sorry for being so crass, but that woman was always saying crazy awful things to you, well before Roy's death. She used to say awful, crazy things to Roy," Courtney said.

"Benny, you were like a deflated ball when you heard the detective's name that was coming to investigate. Picado, I think was his name. You don't like him?" Dana asked.

"You're very perceptive," Benny said, thoroughly impressed.

"Before I sold my soul to public relations, I was an investigative reporter. I'm always reading people, even when I'm trying not to," Dana said, finally mustering a smile.

"His name is Juan Mora Picado, and no, I don't like him. I don't think you'll find anyone in the beach towns around here that likes Picado. He's a jerk and a bully," Benny said.

"Oh, great," Dana said.

"Sorry," Benny replied.

"No need to apologize for telling me the truth. I appreciate that."

"OIJ investigators hate coming to the small beach communities. They feel it's beneath them to make the trip out here. So when they are here, they can be grumpy about it," Benny said.

"So what happens when Skylar accuses me of killing Roy to the detective?"

"Well, he's a jerk, but he is thorough at his job, so regardless of what Skylar says, he'll look at all of us, including Skylar, since usually murders are committed by someone the victim knows. Especially down here. I can't remember the last time there was a murder anywhere around here. Sometimes there is drug-related stuff that happens, but not here. Not murder, at least," Benny said.

Courtney raised her hand in the air and said, "Sorry, crass Courtney here again, but what happens to the whole lawsuit and the contention of the will now that Roy is dead?"

"Well, like in the United States, everything shifts over to the spouse at the time of death, so the suit's principal could be amended to be Skylar, unless she's too distraught and wants to drop the whole thing and go back home," Benny said.

Dana guffawed at the remark and quickly put her hands over her mouth in regret.

But it was too late, all three laughed about it, and for Dana it felt good. She needed to laugh about something on that awful day.

After a few minutes, they all settled down around the kitchen's center island. There was some leftover banana daiquiri in the refrigerator. Courtney took out the pitcher and waved it in the air. "I think we need a drink." Dana agreed.

"It doesn't look like Skylar will give up fighting me over Casa Verde," Dana said wistfully.

Benny nodded. "Seems to me she's doubling down."

Courtney put down three glasses on the counter and poured in the banana daiquiri.

"She's the catalyst behind all this legal drama. I know it," Dana said. She took a sip from her glass, and the ice-cold drink felt refreshing.

"Roy seemed henpecked," Courtney said.

"I always thought if he and I could just talk, without Skylar around, that we could have come to some amicable agreement. I would have been happy to share Casa Verde with him. But Skylar was adamant. And he was in such a financial bind that he must have agreed to all this to get from down under, financially speaking," Dana said. "Especially with a rich, powerful man like Gustavo Barca footing the bills."

"And he's doing so because Roy agreed to sell him Casa Verde?" Courtney asked.

"He's sure not doing it out of the kindness of his heart. If he's footing the bill, he must have a signed contract with Roy and Skylar with this property on the line," Benny said.

"You don't think they killed Roy over this property?" Dana asked. That thought had her crumbling down emotionally.

"We know nothing about anything yet. Let's let the investigators do their work," Benny said.

"Yes, for all we know it was some random thing, a mugging or something like that," Courtney added.

Dana remained quiet.

"Dana, listen, even if this was about the property, his death has nothing to do with you. They shut people out of their parents' wills all the time. Death and the estates left behind are ripe for tearing even close families apart. Throw in an estranged father and son into the mix and I would have been shocked if this estate would have been executed peacefully without a contentious fight breaking out for the property," Benny said.

Dana nodded. "I know that, but thank you for saying it. It's hard to believe that if I had walked away and just let Roy have this property, he might still be alive."

"Don't go there," Courtney said.

Too late, Dana thought.

Wally seemed to materialize out of thin air, and it was like he knew that Dana was feeling sad. He jumped on the counter and then plopped on her lap.

"Who is that?" Benny said. He sounded surprised as he smiled, looking at the white cat on Dana's lap.

"This is Wally. He sort of moved in, I guess," Dana said, smiling at the purring cat.

Benny left at around nine o'clock that evening. Dana and Courtney hung out in their favorite spot of the house, the patio. Wally perched on the porch's railing like he was standing guard.

It was a warm tropical night, but there was a nice sea breeze coming from the Pacific colliding with a misty breeze from the jungle, making it a lovely temperature on the porch, especially with the overhead fan moving the air around.

"I don't think I'm going to make it out here, Courtney. You were right, this is too drastic, too impulsive, and that was before I had to contend with not only a murder, but being accused of it by Skylar, who's probably telling that crabby detective right now that I'm the killer, and I'm in a foreign country to boot. It's getting to be too much. Maybe it's best for me to go back to San Francisco with you," Dana said.

"Nothing would make me happier than you moving back, but not under these circumstances," Courtney said, a strong resolve in her voice that Dana was not used to from her flighty best friend.

Dana looked at her, a bit surprised.

"If you go back, it should be under your own terms, not out of fear," Courtney said, wiping a tear from her eye. "Besides, I'm not leaving here until this stuff is all settled. So, I'm sorry, but you can't hog up this view and keep those howler monkeys and that cat all to yourself."

Dana went to bed at eleven p.m., but it wasn't until around two a.m. that she finally began to drift off to sleep. Off in the distance, a howler monkey did its thing, loudly.

Wally jumped on the bed and kneaded at the sheets by her feet for a while, purring loudly until finally getting his spot just right, and he plopped down next to her. Dana smiled then fell asleep.

THIRTEEN

Dana slept until almost nine in the morning, a rarity for an early riser like her, but she didn't fret about it. She needed the sleep after being awake for almost twenty hours straight. When the body wants to sleep, it will get it.

She went downstairs and Courtney was already up, having a breakfast of cereal with milk, a plate of fruit, and a cup of coffee next to her.

"Morning," she said. Dana greeted her back and poured herself some cereal and a cup of coffee. She began to eat the cereal dry.

"I've been watching you eat cereal without milk since college and it still boggles my mind every time I see you eating it like that...it's cereal blasphemy," Courtney said, breaking out in laughter.

Dana shrugged her shoulders and ate her cereal out of the bowl with her hands like it was popcorn. Dana watched as Wally came running into the kitchen for eggs and bacon. He sniffed around and the smell of dry cereal didn't catch his interest, so he sauntered out towards the living room.

"How are you doing?" Courtney asked, turning serious.

"I'm done feeling sorry for myself. I feel terrible about Roy's death, but I'm not letting Skylar run her mouth about me in my new little community, calling me a murderer. It's not right. I'm here for the long haul, Skylar is not, so I'll do anything I can to help the police catch the killer, but Skylar better knock it off with her vile accusations," Dana said, sounding strong and confident.

"Welcome back," Courtney said, raising her cup of coffee at Dana.

"I can't thank you enough. I would have had a nervous breakdown if you weren't here," Dana said.

"You've helped so many times with my knack for making terrible life decisions over the years, so don't even mention it. I'm just happy I could be here with you and thrilled that you have that determined look in your eyes again," Courtney said.

Dana showered and got dressed. At ten a.m., Benny arrived. He seemed harried as he went inside the house, holding a small briefcase and his laptop messenger bag slung over his shoulder.

He accepted Dana's offer of coffee and the three of them were back sitting around the kitchen center island.

"Picado is in town. He arrived late last night. I called him this morning to let him know you're my client," Benny said.

That statement comforted Dana.

"What did he say?" Courtney asked before Dana could pose the same question.

"He wants to talk to all of us today and get our statements."

"We have nothing to hide," Dana said.

"That is true; however, it's important to understand that the Costa Rican legal system differs greatly from that in America," Benny explained, sounding ominous.

"How different?" Courtney asked.

"Costa Rica follows the French civil code, not the English, so for starters, you don't have the assumption of innocence like you have in America. And although you're not actually assumed guilty, the burden to prove you are not guilty is on you, not the authorities. In America, the prosecutor has to prove you are guilty beyond a reasonable doubt. Here, the fiscal, that's the prosecutor, doesn't have to prove it."

"Yikes," Courtney blurted. Dana took in the information quietly.

"There are more glaring differences."

Oh, brother, Dana thought.

"There is no trial by jury; a trial is presided over by a single judge or by a three-judge panel. And there is no double jeopardy, so even if acquitted, the Ministerio Público, the Public Ministry, can try a person again and again even if they're found not guilty."

"Sheesh, anything else?" Dana asked.

Benny thought for a moment and said, "The Public Ministry and the OIJ can pretty much lock you up at the judicial system's whim using what's called 'preventive detention,' which is a popular strategy they use with foreigners who are deemed flight risks," Benny explained.

"So they can lock someone up without charging them with a crime?" Dana asked.

"Correct. There are a few cases of expats being held for months under preventive detention without having been charged with a crime or even gone to trial. They're locked up while the prosecutor works the case," Benny explained.

Dana and Courtney exchanged a nervous glance.

Dana had agreed to meet the OIJ Investigator at Casa Verde in a couple hours. Benny had provided her a legal briefing on how to handle the interview with the detective.

"We need to find you an attorney," Benny said.

"I have you," Dana replied, blushing. It sounded more personal and intimate than she intended. But she hoped it just sounded that way in her head. He didn't seem to have taken the comment that way, so she felt relieved.

"I practice real estate and business law. The way Skylar is raising a stink to cast you as the perpetrator worries me, so I believe it's prudent to think about bringing in an attorney that specializes in criminal law. I know a few criminal lawyers that I trust, and I'll check to see if they're available so we can have them on standby."

"I don't care how loudly Skylar shouts it, I didn't kill Roy, so I don't need a criminal lawyer, but thank you for your help with this mess."

Benny smiled, but Dana could tell it worried him. And she appreciated it.

Benny drove back to his beach house, which was ten minutes away, to pick up some files he needed. He told Dana he would be back in about forty-five minutes, which would give him plenty of time to get back before Detective Picado's arrival.

Dana refused to sit around twiddling her thumbs, waiting for Agent Picado to arrive, so she jumped on her laptop and sent a text via Messenger to her friend Bucky Moreland back in San Francisco.

I need your help. Are you around?

Bucky replied right away, *Yup what's up?*

Bucky was a software engineer with a pile of degrees and a Ph.D. in computer engineering and mathematics from MIT and Stanford. He made a fortune writing code for unicorn startups in Silicon Valley. In the valley, a unicorn company was a startup tech company that was valued at over a billion dollars. The Ubers and Facebooks of the tech business world.

She had known Bucky for a long time and back when she worked as a reporter. She had interviewed him for a story she was working about the company he was working for that was disrupting some old industry. She couldn't even remember which, since every startup had lobbed on to the whole disrupt mantra regardless of its validity.

She had become friends with Bucky, and whenever she needed to find information about a story she was working on, she could always count on Bucky to help her find the goods. She hadn't needed his help in that regard as much since she had gone into public relations, but he had her on retainer, since most billionaire techies seemed to need the service of a public relations expert at one time or another. Usually for saying or doing something dumb. He had even offered to keep her on retainer as a freelancer when she moved down to Costa Rica, but Dana was adamant that she was finished with that line of work.

Bucky loved helping her out when she needed information about something. It was the work that reminded him of his teen hacker days, he had told her a few years ago.

She had even offered to pay him for his expertise, but he sneered at it, telling her he didn't need the money, that it was just for fun and to help a friend.

Dana tapped on her keyboard.

Need you to work your magic background on someone.

No problem. Name? Bucky replied via text.

Skylar Kirkpatrick, Dana messaged back.

"What are you up to?" Courtney asked. She was eyeing her suspiciously.

"Just asked Bucky to look into something for me," Dana replied.

"Oh, boy. Are you sure that's a good idea? The last thing we need is to tick off that detective," Courtney said.

"Well, I can't sit here doing nothing while Skylar is throwing dirt my way, so let's just see what dirt Bucky can find on her. See how she likes it," Dana said.

"I have two words for you that will keep me up tonight: preventive detention," Courtney said.

"I won't even dwell on the fact that there is a killer on the loose out there and no one seems too concerned about that, so if I can offer the detective a little nudge in the right direction, why not?" Dana said.

"Again, two words: preventive detention," Courtney said. She turned away and walked out to the porch.

Before Dana could say anything, Courtney yelled out, "Benny is here."

"Who opened the gate?" Dana wondered.

Benny parked out front and looked up and saw Dana and Courtney above on the patio. He smiled and waved.

"Come on in," Dana said.

They met downstairs and sat in the living room.

"Did Ramón open the gate for you?" Dana asked.

"Yes. He was doing some yard work by the front gate. He heard me pull up and when he saw it was me, he opened it. Sorry if that was fresh on my part," Benny said.

"Oh, no, not at all," Dana said, feeling awkward, then added, "With everything going on and since there is still a killer out there, I just wanted to make sure there wasn't a problem with the front gate."

"It's good to be security-minded. Ramón only let me in because he knows me, so don't worry that he'll be letting just anyone off the street."

They went into the kitchen and gathered around the island. Dana mused it was becoming their de facto headquarters for serious discussions.

"No cat?" Benny asked, looking around for Wally.

"He's a free spirit, comes and goes," Dana said.

Benny put his briefcase on the countertop.

"This has become our conference room," Dana said, smiling.

"I read somewhere that regardless of the palatial accouterments available, people end up gravitating to the kitchen to talk," Benny said.

Benny provided the latest update on the legal battle for Casa Verde. "I received a call from a powerhouse attorney that is handling the case for Roy. He wanted to let me know that the case was moving forward with Skylar. There will be no slowdowns or delays because of Roy's murder. Skylar wants this resolved and will keep the case going with whatever the OIJ is doing to bring the killer to justice. He was adamant these are two different matters, and Skylar wants nothing to interfere with the real estate feud with you," Benny said.

"That poor grieving widow," Courtney said with an eye roll that was so slow, complete, and dramatic, that Dana cracked up. Benny didn't join in the laugh. He was in legal eagle mode.

"Sorry," Dana said, clearing her throat as Courtney giggled.

"From my interactions with Roy and Skylar, this doesn't surprise me. Seemed like she was the one pushing Roy into this," Benny said.

"What about Roy's body? Will it be difficult to transport him back to the States for burial?" Dana asked. It was a question out of left field that had nothing to do with the legal matters at hand, but it was a question that had been bothering her to think what would happen to her cousin's body.

Benny seemed taken aback by the question. "Well, the body has not been released to Skylar by the authorities yet. Agent Picado had a forensics team from San José come down to process the scene and they were there for a while before they let the coroner remove the body. After that, they transported it to the Medical Examiner's office in San José late last night. Officer Freddy told me that Skylar wanted Roy's body released to her ASAP, and that she planned to cremate him in San José, since it would be too expensive to have the body flown back to the

States. She said it would be a lot cheaper to just bring his ashes in an urn back to the States," Benny said.

"She seems a little eager to have the body cremated, don't you think?" Dana asked.

Benny shrugged his shoulders. He didn't know how to respond to her question, so she changed the subject. "Do you know how he was killed?"

"Officer Freddy told me he was stabbed. But please don't repeat that to anyone outside our little circle. Freddy could get in a world of hurt if Agent Picado finds out he's been telling me stuff about the case on the down low."

"I never reveal my sources," Dana said seriously.

"Mum's the word," Courtney said as she touched the tips of her thumb and index finger, and slid them across her closed mouth in a *my lips are sealed* gesture.

"So, what can I expect from this Detective Picado?" Dana asked.

"A lot of disdain and condescension," Benny replied instantly.

"Fan-Tas-Tic," Dana replied.

"He will ask you about your strained relationship with Roy," Benny said. Dana interrupted him.

"I didn't have a strained relationship with Roy. We really have had little of a family relationship in over ten years," she corrected him.

"Your families have been estranged. You inherited his father's property instead of him. He sued you in California. He sued you here. His widow is telling everyone and their brother and sister that you killed him over the legal dispute. So trust me, in the eyes of the law, you had a strained relationship," Benny said.

"I understand. I get it. I'll try not to sound so defensive when the detective brings that up," Dana said contritely.

Benny smiled and nodded. "Excellent." Then he said, "The investigator will want to know your whereabouts for the time of the murder."

"Well, that's easy, we've been inseparable since we landed in Costa Rica. I can vouch for her," Courtney said.

After going over a few more details about the case, Dana, Benny, and Courtney moved over to the living room area to wait for the police to arrive.

They didn't say much. A few minutes later, the front door buzzer screamed to life, causing all three of them to jump in their seats.

FOURTEEN

Agent Picado arrived on time, and it didn't take long for him to live up to his surly reputation. He barely shook Dana's hand and only did so because she left it in the air, forcing him to acknowledge it and shake it. He shrugged at Benny and Courtney.

There were two other people with him whom he did not bother to introduce.

There was a woman who seemed to be in her early thirties. She wore a black open blazer and pants. Her hair was black, and she wore it in a professional low ponytail. She was beautiful.

The woman seemed to wait for Picado to introduce her, but when he wandered into the living room looking around the house, she took it upon herself to introduce herself.

"I'm Detective Gabriela Rojas, an investigator with the OIJ in Nicoya," she said.

"Junior detective," Picado said dismissively with his back to everyone as he continued to look around.

Rojas rolled her eyes and gave Dana a *see what I have to put up with* look. Unlike Picado, she seemed nice, Dana thought.

The third person was a blond-haired, fair-skinned man that looked American to Dana.

"I'm Adam Mitchell with the United States Embassy."

"The Embassy?" a surprised Dana asked.

"The OIJ is kind enough to let an embassy official sit in when they question American citizens, and they keep us in the loop when a U.S. citizen dies in their country. So we're two for two in this case," Mitchell explained nervously.

Mitchell seemed unsure of himself and his role in the proceedings, which couldn't be more polar opposite than the way Picado presented himself. There was no doubt Picado was in charge and that Mitchell was intimidated, if not downright frightened of him. Picado immediately took charge of the meeting.

"I'm the senior homicide detective in this area and the lead investigator into the murder of Mr. Roy Kirkpatrick," Picado said. "Mr. Mitchell is here as a courtesy, and he's only here to observe. If you have questions about these proceedings, you ask me, not him."

Dana could see Adam Mitchell cower. Picado had ratcheted up the tension to its breaking point in less than five minutes. He had yet to ask her a single question. Dana turned to look at Courtney, who looked terrified. Dana smiled at her. She would not let this man intimidate her.

Detective Picado was in his fifties. He was thin and tall, with dark skin, short black hair, and piercing black eyes. He had a thick black mustache that was so black, it seemed dyed.

They all sat in Dana's living room, and for the next forty-five minutes, he held court as he asked Dana and Benny about the lawsuit and the fight over Casa Verde.

"You don't think Roy's death has anything to do with this property?" Dana asked.

Picado scoffed. "This is a very valuable property. I've seen people killed over a shot of guaro."

"Well, I don't even know what guaro is, but I had nothing to do with his death."

Picado looked at her dismissively.

"Guaro is a very strong drink here. Kind of like tequila," Mitchell said sheepishly.

"It's more like rubbing alcohol than tequila," Benny interjected.

"That is not important," Picado barked. "All I'm saying is that I've seen people killed for something far less valuable than this property."

He turned his attention to Courtney, and Dana could see her best friend tense up.

"And you are a friend of Ms. Kirkpatrick from San Francisco. Courtney Lowe, correct?"

"Yes," Courtney replied.

Finished with generalities and background questions, Picado got down to it.

"It does not appear that the motive for the murder of Mr. Kirkpatrick was robbery or drug-related, which are usually the reasons for killings around here. So when I asked Mrs. Skylar Kirkpatrick if she could think of anyone that might have wanted her husband dead, she brought up your name immediately. Now, why would she say something like that?" Picado asked.

"First of all, it's not true. Roy was my cousin, and no matter what happened between us, I would never want him hurt or killed. But like you've said, we are involved in a legal dispute over this property, but I would never resort to killing a human being for anything, especially over something so trivial as a piece of property. I don't care how valuable it is," Dana said.

"That's not what Skylar Kirkpatrick thinks," Picado said. He stared at Dana's face closely. Dana knew the technique. It was one they had taught her in journalism school and a technique she had honed well over the years. It was a great skill to try to see if the interviewee's face gave off a tell that showed if the person was lying.

"I can't imagine what she's going through, losing her husband, and we have been involved in this property dispute, and although Roy and I weren't close anymore, there was never animosity between us. Skylar never liked me, so I guess that's why she's saying such horrible and vicious things about me, which let me be clear to you once again, Detective Picado, her accusations are one hundred percent not true. I had nothing to do with my cousin's death," Dana said.

Picado looked down and began jotting into a pocket-sized notebook.

Benny leaned back and smiled. Dana smiled back. She knew she was handling the ill-tempered detective well. She wasn't letting him rattle her cage.

Picado scribbled away in his notebook for a few more seconds in silence. The whole room fell into silence. Then he looked back up at Dana and said, "Mr. Kirkpatrick was killed at eleven thirty p.m. on Sunday. Where were you that night?" Picado asked.

"Right here. Well, upstairs in my bedroom, asleep," Dana said.

"I can vouch for that. We even slept in the same bed," Courtney chimed in without being asked.

Picado raised an eyebrow and looked at her. Courtney looked around and noticed everyone else had skewed their attention to her.

"Because of those loud monkeys raising Cain all night, they scared me," Courtney explained.

Dana blushed and said, "Actually, Courtney, on that night we slept in our own separate rooms."

"So if you both were asleep in separate rooms on the night of the murder, then you can't say with certainty that either of you remained in that room from the time you last saw each other that night until the next morning when you saw each other again. Isn't that correct?" Picado asked.

"Well, yeah, but—" Dana tried to speak, but she was cut off by Picado.

"Thank you, that is all for now," he said.

As the detectives and Adam Mitchell prepared to leave, Picado turned around at the front door to face Dana. With a steely glare and stern voice, he said, "You're not allowed to leave the country while this investigation is ongoing."

"I moved here, so I'm not planning on leaving anytime soon," Dana said, feeling defiant.

"If you leave the Nosara area, you need to call Detective Rojas and let her know where you're going and how long you'll be away from Mariposa Azul Beach. I don't care if you're going to the next town over or up to San José, you must let us know. Is that understood?"

"I understand. No problem," Dana answered calmly.

"Mind if I talk to you for a few minutes?" Adam Mitchell asked as Picado and Rojas walked outside.

Ramón was out front with a machete cutting yuca. Dana watched Picado walking over to him with his notebook in hand and begins talking to him. She couldn't hear what he was saying, but Picado pointed in her direction.

"Seems like I'm the prime suspect," Dana said.

"Not necessarily. Picado enjoys making everyone he interviews squirm into thinking they're a suspect," Benny said.

"Well, it worked," Dana said.

Mitchell fidgeted with his tie.

"So what's your role here, Mr. Mitchell?" Dana asked.

"I'm afraid there isn't much we can do in these types of situations. We don't have jurisdiction here, and even though you're a U.S. citizen, you're under Costa Rican law, not U.S. I can try to facilitate communication and observe the process to ensure it's fair, but only from a third-party observer status," Mitchell said.

"Well, that inspires all sorts of warm, fuzzy feelings," Courtney said.

"Sorry. But as an embassy representative, I'm here as a courtesy of the OIJ. I'm sure you know by now that they are the Judicial Investigation Department unit of the Supreme Court of Justice for Costa Rica. We had to lean hard on the powers that be in San José to even let me sit in on this interview. I just want to make sure you understand that the role of the Embassy here is limited, but the ambassador knows of what's going on and she's following the case closely. I'll be reporting back to her tomorrow," Mitchell said.

"You're leaving?" Dana asked.

"Yes, I'm going back to San José tonight. It's good you have a local attorney to help you," Mitchell said, looking over at Benny. "If you're arrested, the OIJ will let me know and I'll be available if you have questions," Mitchell said.

Dana and Courtney's eyes grew wide. "Arrest me?"

"I don't mean to frighten you, just covering all the bases, and Costa Rica has a law similar to our Miranda Rights, where you can abstain from providing a statement without your attorney, so don't be hoodwinked into thinking you don't have that protection. You do, so don't say anything without talking to your lawyer first. If for whatever reason you need another attorney, let me know," Mitchell said, handing Dana his business card.

"I have calls out to top-notch criminal attorneys," Benny said.

"Anyway, call me if you have questions," Mitchell said as he stepped outside. "They're my ride back to town, so I have to go," he said, walking towards the white sedan.

Picado seemed to be finished talking with Ramón, as he was

getting into the front passenger side of the car. Rojas was behind the wheel and Mitchell quickly climbed in the back. They drove with Picado on his cell phone.

Courtney hugged Dana.

"I'm fine," Dana said. "Skylar, Picado, that embassy guy, they're actually starting to tick me off."

"Uh-oh, that's trouble," Courtney said.

"Please do not repeat that outside of present company," Benny said, smiling nervously.

FIFTEEN

Dana was still fuming about her encounter with Detective Picado when her phone buzzed. It was Bucky Moreland, her tech genius friend from San Francisco.

For a moment she had forgotten she had reached out to him for help. But as soon as she saw his name on her phone's screen, she excitedly took the call. They exchanged quick hellos, and he got right into it.

"I found out some interesting information about Roy and Skylar," he said, sounding mischievous. "He had filed for divorce three times in the last two years, but he stopped the divorce procedures every time. The last time he filed for divorce was just four months ago."

"And then a month later they came down here," Dana said.

"They're also broke. And I mean b-r-o-k-e...those two owe money to everyone and their brother to the tune of over one hundred thousand dollars in debt, with maxed-out credit cards, and they're being evicted for not paying rent in months."

"Wow. No wonder they're so eager to contest Uncle Blake's will and come down here to stay at a five-star resort for free."

Bucky told Dana he would email her some documents, and

the two friends said goodbye. Dana thanked him for his help. After the call with Bucky, Dana filled Courtney in with all the details as she opened the email and clicked on an attachment.

"Here is the info he said he was sending," Dana said as she sat quietly for a couple minutes, looking it over. "Yikes. I'm stressed out just thinking about living a day under the financial mess those two got themselves into," Dana said, reading the document. "Hmm, this is interesting."

"What did you find?" Courtney said, coming around to look over Dana's shoulder.

"Well, since Skylar is so adamant to shout from the rooftops that I killed Roy, I thought maybe she was trying to deflect people like in that old dice under the cup to get everyone to look at the wrong cup," Dana said.

"And you're the wrong cup," Courtney said.

"Exactly. She has a fat life insurance policy on Roy, so no matter how the lawsuit for this property plays out, she has a nice chunk of change coming her way now that Roy is dead."

"How much?" Courtney asked.

"One million bucks," Dana replied.

Courtney whistled. "That should take care of those debts and leave her with a nice cushion. What about this property dispute?"

"I guess if I lose the legal battle she gets it, but that's a big if, according to Benny. And I already beat them in the States, so it's not looking good here, so she's looking at going back home empty-handed with all that debt waiting for her. Their marriage was on the rocks. But with Roy dead, she's going back to a million dollars all for herself."

"Sounds like a good motive to me," Courtney said.

"Me too. Another bonus for her, by killing Roy in Costa Rica, she doesn't have to deal with the U.S. legal system and cops," Dana said.

Benny arrived about an hour later. Dana had emailed him the documents Bucky had sent her right away, so he was caught up on that front.

It surprised Dana that he wasn't too keen on her snooping like that.

"It's really best if we let the authorities do their thing. The last thing we need is for Picado to get wind of your snooping on Skylar like this and he'll blow his top at your meddling," Benny said.

"Meddling? I'm being accused of being a murderer, and it seems like the cops believe it enough to look into it, so why shouldn't I be proactive?" Dana said. She knew she was coming off emotional, hurt, and angry, but she didn't care. *It's my life*, she thought.

"I'm just worried about how this might be perceived by Picado. He always has a huge chip on his shoulder, but when Americans are involved, it adds another ton or two to that chip. I wouldn't take Picado checking you out too personally. It's what cops everywhere in the world do when someone is killed and they're investigating. They will always start close to home, then they fan out, so he'll be looking at everyone: the spouse, the family, friends, business dealings. Picado might be a jerk, but he is a good detective. I'm sure he's looking at Skylar. He'll find out about that life insurance. Heck, I'm sure he's even looking at Courtney and me. For cops, everyone inside the family circle is a suspect until they can rule them out."

"Dana, the last thing you want is to get Picado riled up so he puts you under that preventive detention so you can't impede this investigation," Courtney said.

"And not to be disrespectful about Roy's death, but I just heard from Skylar's lawyer and she's pushing even harder in contesting the will now than when Roy was alive. So she is not taking time off to grieve, so we need to focus on that, first and foremost," Benny said.

"What did her lawyer say?" Dana asked.

"Not to expect any delays or reprieves. Roy's death changes nothing, so we proceed with the case just as before," Benny said.

"Cold," Courtney said.

Dana and Benny nodded in agreement when the front doorbell rang. She quickly shut down her laptop as if to hide the documents Bucky had emailed her just in case Picado was out front.

"It's Ramón," Benny said, looking down from the porch.

Dana welcomed Ramón inside. He was wearing his ever-present work coveralls, making Dana wonder if had more than one set. He was holding on to his field hat with both hands. Dana, Ramón, and Benny spoke in Spanish.

"What is it?" Dana asked him.

Ramón was apologetic for answering Picado's questions about Dana.

"It's okay, Ramón, I don't want you to get in trouble," Dana said.

"What did he ask you?" Benny asked.

"He asked us questions about the night that Don Roy died," Ramón said.

"What kinds of questions?" Dana asked.

"He wanted to know if we saw or heard you or anyone else leave the house any time after ten o'clock on the night Don Roy was killed. We told him no. The car was there all night, and we didn't hear anyone coming or leaving. Then he asked if someone could leave the house at night without us knowing. I said sure, through the back pathway leading towards town, but that we would have probably heard the gate open and close. But not always," Ramón said, looking down at the white ceramic tile in the entryway's floor.

"It's okay, Ramón. I have nothing to hide," Dana said.

Ramón nodded and left.

Dana looked at Benny.

"Like I told you before, this is routine stuff the police do when investigating a crime."

"Still makes me feel queasy inside. I've never been subjected to anything like this in my entire life. It's unnerving. Regardless of how routine it might be to ask those types of questions, it's scaring me," Dana said.

SIXTEEN

Dana found it hard to believe it was just her fourth day in the Mariposa Beach community. She stood on her porch with a cup of coffee, looking around the property. Wally was sleeping, taking the entire couch for his tiny little body.

When Dana first arrived, she had been taken aback by what she perceived to be the over-the-top fortification of the property by Uncle Blake.

A ten-foot rock wall surrounded the property. If that wasn't enough to dissuade intruders, they encrusted the top of the wall with shards of broken glass in case an agile burglar got any ideas of climbing the wall and jumping over it.

Then there was that unwelcoming green electric front gate that remained tightly closed at all times.

Access to Casa Verde was restricted and granted on a case-by-case basis, managed and controlled via the intercom radio setup.

But that wasn't done because of an imminent danger, it was just how they designed homes for preventive reasons compared to the States; it was a bit much, but in Costa Rica, Casa Verde had the security offerings desired by homeowners.

Especially at Mariposa Beach, where the closest police substation was twenty minutes away.

Dana also had a second line of defense: Ramón. He seemed to always be busy outside with landscaping work.

So although at first it seemed like overkill, she appreciated the level of security Casa Verde offered her and Courtney.

The last thing Dana wanted to do was leave the safe zone of Casa Verde. And it wasn't the safety it offered from the killer but from loose lips in town.

She knew the community was bubbling with gossip about her, Skylar, Uncle Blake, and her murdered cousin, Roy. The gossipy old ladies, appropriately given the nickname of the Gossip Brigade, who gathered at Qué Vista in the morning for Bloody Marys and a game of canasta, must have their lips working overtime with all the juicy new gossip that had come to town since Dana had moved in.

But she was not one to live in self-imposed house arrest; Mariposa Beach was her new home, and she wasn't planning on living in fear, secluded and hidden away. So against Courtney and Benny's advice, they went out for dinner and drinks out on the town.

"Are you sure about this?" Courtney asked.

"No. But let's go anyway."

Benny took them to Ike's Oceanview, a restaurant he had recommended before the whole ugly mess with Roy's murder had happened.

Oceanview was located a couple miles up the mountain, nestled in the forest. The restaurant offered breathtaking views of the ocean down below. It was fancier than the on-beach setting of the Qué Vista Restaurant in town. But fancy in Mariposa Beach didn't mean stuffy or having to dress up. Dana loved that it seemed a big rule of living in a small beach community was that you dressed casual and comfortable.

Dana and Courtney wore sundresses. Benny wore jeans and a polo shirt, and that's as dressed up as you got in Mariposa Beach.

They pulled up into the restaurant, and it was a sight to see. It reminded Dana of Tara from *Gone with the Wind*.

"That is a lovely building. Looks more like an estate than a restaurant," Dana mused as she got out of the car.

Benny explained that Ike Van de Berg was a Dutchman who had moved to Costa Rica in the late 1970s. He bought a lot of land around Mariposa Beach when it was still cheap, and he opened his restaurant in the mid-80s. It did good business, but the land it sat on was now worth a fortune. Ike was pushing seventy, so if he ever retired and sold his land, he'd be set until he was around three hundred fifty years old, Benny had explained to Dana and Courtney, smiling.

"Welcome," Ike said loudly as the trio walked in.

Dana smiled. He was a big man, shaved head. He looked like the late actor Donald Pleasence from *Halloween*. He wore a white guayabera shirt and tan pants. Although it was the first time Dana met him, she figured he already knew who she was from how he greeted her.

"I hope last night's tragedy doesn't put you off our little beach community and that you're enjoying that beautiful home that is Casa Verde," he said warmly, then quickly added, "Oh, and I'm so sorry for your loss, even though your cousin and that wife of his were insufferable. I was about to ban them from my restaurant. Sorry, no offense."

Dana smiled. It was the first she had laid eyes on Ike, and he knew all about her and those were his first words to her...all in two breaths.

"Thank you for the warm welcome, and no offense taken," Dana said, smiling.

She wanted to say she agreed with Ike's assessment of Roy

and Skylar, but Benny would have had a coronary, since he kept reminding her not to talk to anyone about the case.

Dana appreciated that Ike wasn't making her feel like an unwelcome killer. Far from it. Ike sat them at the best table he had available, and the three of them enjoyed a delicious meal and a bottle of red wine from Chile.

"Like I told you before, most people here are wonderful. Like any other place on Earth, you have good people and bad people," Benny said.

"With an unknown murderer running wild out there," Dana said.

"Well, yes, there is that matter that needs to be resolved, and that's where we wash our hands and let the police do their work."

The food was amazing.

Dana ordered the arroz con pollo—a rice and chicken dish that was very popular in Costa Rica. It looked like a Chinese rice stir-fry dish.

Courtney ordered the arroz con mariscos—seafood rice dish. They both came with a side salad, fried plantains, and French fries.

Benny ordered the pescado entero—the whole fish, and it wasn't an exaggeration. From head to tail, the entire fish was on his plate. Its eyes stared at Dana as she ate her meal.

After a few minutes, Dana said, "Sorry, I can't eat with your meal eyeballing me." She grabbed a napkin and gently placed it over the fish's head. She sat and looked at her handiwork. "There. Much better," she said, sighing before all three of them broke out in laughter.

The lighthearted moment and the fun evening out was just what Dana needed, and then Gustavo Barca showed up.

SEVENTEEN

Dana had heard so much about Gustavo Barca in the few days since she had moved to Mariposa Beach, and much of it was not good. She half expected him to be some ominous-looking fiend.

Instead, he looked...*well, normal*, she thought.

He was a stout, middle-aged man. Short, at around five-five. He had a round face, skin with a warm, golden-brown tint, and he was bald. Short, stocky, and bald, but by the way he carried himself, he was a seven-foot-tall Adonis. He oozed confidence as he made his way through the restaurant, glad-handing diners and staff like a politician at the state fair.

Dana was like a deer caught in the headlights, and she became mortified when Barca looked at her and his thin lips spread into a big smile. He gave her an acknowledging nod, and he made his way to their table.

"He's heading our way," Dana said under her breath. "It's like staring at Medusa, I couldn't look away and now here he comes..."

"Miss Kirkpatrick, nice to meet you. I'm Gustavo Barca."

"Seems like everyone knows who I am," Dana said without saying hello.

Barca laughed. "It's a small town, word travels fast."

"I've heard that a few times," Dana said.

Dana shook his hand because he wasn't putting it down until she did, so she didn't want to be rude.

"Hello, Mr. Barca," Dana said coldly.

"Please, call me Gustavo," he said, making direct eye contact.

Barca greeted Benny warmly with a handshake and he shook Courtney's hand and introduced himself to her, as well.

"Please accept my condolences for your uncle's death. He was a fine man," Barca said, turning solemn.

"Thanks," Dana said. She doubted he was being sincere, but he was being polite, so she would do the same.

"I really think we should talk in the next few days. I'll call Benny here to set something up," Barca said.

"I'm not interested in selling the property," Dana replied.

"We'll leave that for another day. Enjoy your dinner," Barca said as he walked away.

"That was weird," Courtney said.

"The man is always working an angle. I'm actually curious what he has up his sleeve," Benny said.

"I'm sure we'll find out soon enough. The man has been a thorn in my side since I inherited Casa Verde," Dana said, returning to her dinner.

Soon enough, Gustavo Barca was out of their mind as they ate, chatted, and laughed. The pitcher of margaritas went down so smoothly between the three of them that they ordered a second one.

They each had tres leches for dessert, and by nine o'clock, Dana, feeling the margaritas, was feeling exhausted.

She had always been one of those early to bed, early to rise types, which had always annoyed her ex-husband. *Why are you thinking about him?* she thought.

"I know I'm coming off like an old lady, but I've hit the wall, can we go home?" Dana asked.

"Of course," Benny said, waving his hand in the air for the check.

The waiter came over and said, "Mr. Barca picked up the check for your table before he left. You're all set."

Benny, Dana, and Courtney looked at each other with surprise.

"Dang, we should have ordered some food to take home, and more margaritas," Courtney said in jest as Dana and Benny laughed.

The next morning, Dana was slower at getting up than usual. At first, she couldn't remember why she had overslept and why she felt so groggy.

"Oh, yeah, those pitchers of margaritas. Such a lightweight," she said out loud to her empty bedroom.

She looked down at the end of the bed and there was Wally curled up asleep.

"Good morning, Wally," she said as she got out of bed.

In the bathroom, she splashed some cold water on her face for about a minute and she brushed her teeth. She stood there in front of the mirror for a moment, checking her tired-looking face.

"Coffee. You need coffee, stat," she said to herself, yawning.

After breakfast and a long, relaxing bath, Dana was ready to tackle the world. She would not think about Agent Picado, Gustavo Barca, Skylar, dead Cousin Roy, Casa Verde, or her legal quandaries. She was excited to take out the Willys Jeep into her new living area beyond Casa Verde and the beach town.

"You know this is our fifth day here and we haven't explored these parts," Dana said in passing during breakfast.

"You're right," Courtney said.

"Well, we're changing that today," Dana said. She was excited and eager to take out that funky little red Willys Jeep to explore and go off-roading.

"Yikes," Courtney said.

EIGHTEEN

"Are you sure we won't get in trouble with the police for leaving town?" Courtney asked Dana as they climbed onto the Jeep.

Detective Picado had warned them not to leave town.

"Benny called the police to let them know we were going to Nosara and would be back in a couple hours, so we're fine."

Dana was impressed how well the almost seventy-year-old red Willys Jeep handled the narrow winding roads between Mariposa Beach and Nosara.

"I'm amazed how well this little Jeep handles the road," Dana said.

"I'm amazed we haven't plummeted off the mountainside," a wary Courtney said.

Dana laughed as she pressed down on the accelerator.

"Slow down, you're Dana Kirkpatrick, not Danica Patrick!" Courtney begged as she white-knuckled the door sidebar grip.

Dana smiled then slowed down and pulled over to the side of the road to take in the breathtaking views of the Pacific Ocean below.

It reminded Dana of California State Route 1—a similar winding north–south state highway that ran along the Pacific coastline of California, offering stunning views of the coastline from San Francisco to Los Angeles.

"Beautiful," Dana said, staring out to the Pacific.

"It sure is," Courtney agreed.

After a moment of taking it all in, they got back in the Willys and Dana noticed a dirt road off the highway that appeared to head up into the mountains.

"Ooh, off-roading," she said as she started up the Willys and made a sharp right turn, then crossed the road onto the shoulder and then up the steep path leading into the jungle.

"Um, Dana, I'm not sure that this is such a good idea in a seventy-year-old jalopy," Courtney said.

"Bite your tongue, Big Red is in amazing shape," Dana said.

"Big Red?"

"Yeah, I'm christening her Big Red. Don't worry, Benny said this was my uncle's pride and joy. Shipped it down from the States. He completely refurbished it. Disc brakes and electric ignition, so we don't even need to use the hand crank to start it unless we really need to," Dana said, smiling.

"Hand crank? What are you even talking about?" Courtney said as she adjusted the seatbelt across her chest.

"I think that's as tight as the seatbelt gets," Dana said, looking over at Courtney as Big Red whirred up the hillside, over some fallen branches and through the forest. It didn't look like an official road but more of a narrow path that was very drivable until Dana had to slam on the breaks at a river crossing.

"Okay, fun is over, make a U-turn and let's get back on the main road. I never thought I would say this, but I miss those potholes," Courtney said.

"It's not that deep," Dana said, looking over the dashboard at the water.

"Don't even go there, Dana!"

"This is a real Army Jeep from the forties and fifties. Built to handle obstacles like a river crossing any day of the week, and twice on Sundays," Dana said, looking over to the right and then to the left.

"Please, turn this thing around and let's get back on the real road," Courtney pleaded.

Dana looked at the crossing. The water was calm. It really didn't look too deep. And it was a clear, sunny day. The path was very dry. Dana knew they were still in the dry season, so it probably hadn't rained in a while. If it had, the dirt road would be mud and the river would be ferocious.

"Stop thinking about it! Let's go back," Courtney said.

"Hold on," Dana said.

"Don't you dare."

Dana stepped on the accelerator and slowly drove the Jeep into the water. Once moving, she stepped on the gas and didn't let off until she made it to the other side.

It took less than a minute to clear the waterlogged crossing, and Dana and Courtney screamed the whole time, Dana in delight and Courtney in fear.

Once they made it to the other side, Dana stopped to look back at the river and she yelped. "Now *that* was fun!"

"Don't. Ever. Do. That. Again," Courtney said.

Dana would learn later that that off-road path was a nifty shortcut up to Nosara. It was not one to be toyed with as lightly as she had done, especially during the rainy season that was a couple months away from starting in November.

They made it to Nosara a lot quicker thanks to Dana's off the beaten path adventure. They drove around the area known as Bocas de Nosara, Mouths of Nosara. The locals called it El Pueblo, The Town.

This is where the public schools, the library, and the municipal facilities like the rural police force and ICE—the government-owned public utilities company—were located, along with local banks, a large grocery store, and retail stores for the locals who could never afford to shop in the retail stores down by the beaches. Only the curious foreigners like Dana made their way to El Pueblo.

It was the part of town where the staff in the resorts a few miles down the coast lived.

"*A Tale of Two Cities*," Dana said as they drove through it.

She slammed the brakes, causing Courtney's head to jerk forward.

"Hey, I'm going to need a chiropractor after riding with you in this contraption," Courtney said, rubbing the back of her neck.

"Sorry, but look," Dana said, pointing towards the sidewalk.

Blonde tourists in El Pueblo stuck out like a strobe light at night, so it was easy for Dana to spot Skylar walking on a crowded sidewalk.

Dana backed up the Jeep around the corner, since Big Red also stood out in a crowd.

From that vantage point, they could see Skylar walking next to a short, stocky, bald man.

"Hey, that's the man that paid for our dinner last night," Courtney said.

"Gustavo Barca," Dana said.

The two of them seemed involved in a heated discussion as they made their way down the sidewalk before disappearing inside a three-story building and out of sight.

"Well, he has been Roy and Skylar's sugar daddy," Courtney said.

"Yeah, but she's staying at his five-star resort. I wonder what they're doing over here, together," Dana said.

Courtney shrugged.

They waited for ten minutes. It was hot, and the soft top of the Jeep was rolled down, so Dana felt like an ant under a magnifying glass.

"Dana, I'm boiling up here, let's go," Courtney said.

After another minute or two, Dana agreed, and she fired up the Jeep and drove away.

The drive back was not fun and light like the dive over to Nosara had been. Seeing Skylar and Barca together brought back all the bad energy and worry that had become part of Dana's life because Gustavo Barca wanted Casa Verde.

The whole idea to move to Costa Rica was to start over, to start fresh. But she had to deal with a dead cousin, his ticked-off widow, a suspicious detective, and a greedy developer who wanted to take her property away from her so he could bulldoze it and absorb it into his fancy resort.

There was no way Dana would allow that to happen.

NINETEEN

The next day, Benny came over to Casa Verde in the morning. Ramón was watering the garden and opened the front gate for him. Benny saw Carmen hanging up laundry on a wire clothesline. She smiled and waved as Benny drove up to the house.

Dana was outside on the second-floor deck on her favorite chair. She was reading a paperback from her uncle's massive book collection when she heard the crunching sound of the Land Cruiser's tires on the gravel driveway. She got up and looked down at the carport where Benny parked next to the Willys Jeep.

Dana couldn't help but notice that Big Red looked like a matchbox toy car next to the bulking Land Cruiser.

"Good morning," she said to Benny from above.

He looked up and saw her standing there. They exchanged smiles, and Dana realized she had had little to smile about that morning, but seeing Benny standing down there made her feel happy inside, and that worried her.

"Morning. I brought coffee and bagels from Mindy's," Benny said, holding up the goods as proof.

"Coffee *and* bagels? You may enter," Courtney said with a smile as she opened the front door.

Benny walked in and Courtney stopped him and whispered, "She's feeling a bit down this morning. We saw Skylar and Gustavo Barca yesterday in Nosara. *Together.*"

Benny winced. Courtney nodded in silent agreement.

She escorted Benny upstairs to the deck.

Dana and Benny exchanged an awkward friendly hug. Dana could feel her heart beating stronger as Benny hugged, but she reminded herself that hugging and kissing on the cheek was a common greeting among friends in Costa Rica. *Nothing to it.*

"So, did you have a good time with the jeep?"

Dana's eyes lit up, and she began talking excitedly to Benny about going off-road and the river crossing and all the fun times she and Courtney were having with Big Red—although Courtney made sure to interrupt. "*Fun* isn't really the right word to describe it. *Terrifying* seems more appropriate."

"Big Red?" Benny asked.

Dana told him about the jeep's new nickname.

"I told you that was a great little vehicle," Benny said, nodding his head over towards Big Red parked in the carport down below.

"Anyway, it *was* fun going off-road with Big Red, don't listen to Courtney." She shrugged whimsically, her eyes crinkling at her best friend. "Well, it *was* fun until we ran into Skylar, who was hanging around with Gustavo Barca in Nosara."

"It might not be as odd as you think. Barca has an office in Nosara that handles the administrative stuff for the resort, human resources, accounting, that type of thing," Benny explained. "And he is bankrolling her stay here, so I would expect they have a lot to talk about, especially since my sources at the resort tell me that Skylar is not just hard to handle, but she's quite the spender."

"They seemed to be arguing. Money causes a lot of arguments," Dana said.

"Intriguing, but remember that Skylar seems to argue with just about everyone she interacts with daily. She has the personality that thrives on drama in her life, so she's always looking for it," Benny said.

"What are you reading?" Benny asked, looking at the book on the table.

"*Rum Punch* by Elmore Leonard. It's from my uncle's collection," Dana replied.

The three of them ate bagels and drank coffee, which energized her some.

Dana could see on Benny's face that he wanted to share something unpleasant with her, so once they were finished eating, she told him, "What's up? I can see it on your face. More bad news?"

Benny smiled sheepishly. "You're very intuitive."

"You never really stop being a journalist."

It was Benny's turn to share what he had been up to the day before, and he told Dana how he bumped into Picado in town, so he asked him about the investigation.

"He's cleared Skylar."

"What?"

"He told me her alibi checks out and they cleared her."

"What about the multiple divorce filings from Roy and the big life insurance policy she is set to cash in from? Did you tell him about that?"

"He knew all of that. He has been very thorough in his investigation and it just doesn't seem to point to Skylar being the killer."

"If not her, then who is he looking at now?"

"I asked him, but he basically told me to go fly a kite, since he would not share that information about an active investigation. Especially..." Benny stopped talking abruptly, and he looked out towards the Pacific Ocean.

"Especially what, Benny?"

He hemmed and hawed for a moment.

"Just tell me."

"I asked him if he had also cleared you, and he said no. You're still under suspicion."

"Oh, that's just peachy," Dana said, lying down flat on the chaise lounge. She lay flat on her back, looking up at the ceiling fan.

Right on cue, as if the cat could sense that Dana was feeling sad, Wally sauntered onto the chair and jumped onto Dana's chest and snuggled her.

He made Dana feel better, and she then told herself to stop feeling sorry for herself. She sat back up, Wally lying down on her lap.

"I don't care much for Skylar, but I'm relieved she didn't kill Roy," Dana said, petting Wally like Don Corleone in *The Godfather*.

Courtney looked at Benny and shrugged.

"Picado was probably just playing mind games with me because I was sticking my nose in his case. He loves to rattle cages," Benny said.

"Consider my cage rattled," Dana said, scratching Wally behind his ears as he purred loudly.

Benny left shortly after. He had to make a few calls for work.

By midafternoon, Dana was crawling the walls, so she headed outside towards Big Red as Courtney came running out after her.

"Where are you going?" Courtney asked, out of breath.

"I'm going to Barca's resort," Dana said.

"Honey, that's not a good idea. Benny said it was best to stay put until he looked at what Skylar and Barca were doing in Nosara. Remember, there is a killer out there, and it could very well be Skylar," Courtney said.

"Not according to Picado," Dana said in frustration.

"I don't care what he thinks. And you're in her way of getting even more money with this property," Courtney replied.

"I'm done feeling sorry for myself and I'm not one to cower, so I'm going up there to see what is going on. If Skylar is there, and she wants to make a federal case about me being at the resort, so be it," Dana said.

"Fine, but I'm coming with you."

"Suit yourself," Dana said, even though inside she was happy that Courtney was coming along. *It's good to have a friend in your corner. Just in case things escalate out of control.*

TWENTY

Dana drove on an unpaved road from Casa Verde to the resort. She looked around, thinking how that entire area was what Barca badly wanted to own for his real estate empire.

On the way, she saw a sign for the Pancha Sabhai Institute, the yogi retreat and ashram that Barca also wanted to bulldoze.

"I think we need to stop at the institute for some meditation," Courtney said.

"Couldn't hurt," Dana said, not stopping.

Just beyond the institute was a small farm.

"What a cute little place. It looks like Ramón and Carmen's place," Courtney said.

"That's because they're also campesinos, local farmers. Benny told me that these small campesino farms were quickly disappearing in rural areas. And how at one time all this was all farmland. Once the campesinos were too old to work the land, or they had passed on and their kids moved to town, they began to parcel out the land and sell it. And who could blame them? Making a living farming is tough anywhere in the world. Selling land is easier and more lucrative," Dana said.

A few minutes later, Dana saw the sign for the Tranquil Bay

Resort. While the sign for the institute was small, *blink and you'll miss it*, Barca's sign jutted out of the countryside, towering over Big Red and casting a long, ominous shade onto the road.

"Well, you can't miss that sign. I'll give him that," Courtney said.

Dana turned right and suddenly the bumpy, rough-and-tumble unpaved road turned into a nicely paved road.

"I miss nice roads like this one," Courtney said, looking around.

"That's because we're on Barca's private property now. Unlike the Nosara Districts and all the other districts in the Nicoya Municipality, he has the money to put in a nice, smooth road up to the resort for his guests," Dana said.

They drove on the well-maintained palm tree–lined road for about a minute until they reached a front gate manned by security guards. The guard stepped out of the security shack and looked at the Willys Jeep. He seemed unimpressed.

"He's probably only used to new, nicer cars and won't let us in," Courtney said.

"Don't you listen to her, Big Red," Dana said, caressing the steering wheel.

Dana stopped. The guard leaned in, peering inside, and seeing the two obvious foreigners, one brunette and one blonde, he cracked a smile.

"Are you guests at the resort?" the guard asked in decent English.

"No. We heard there is a great restaurant here, so we wanted to eat there and to check out the resort for our next trip," Dana lied.

"Okay, drive forward to the valet station," the guard said, stepping out of the way. He leaned into the guard station and pressed a button that lifted the barrier arm, granting them access to the posh resort.

"Thank you," Dana and Courtney said in unison as Dana drove up towards the front entrance of the resort.

"That was easy," Courtney said.

"They're not going to turn away a couple of gringas," Dana said with a snort.

"What a dump," Courtney said facetiously as they drove up to the beautiful and swanky resort.

Dana pulled into a wide porte cochère area off the front entrance of the lobby. A couple of valets and a bellhop greeted them warmly.

"Beautiful jeep, miss. A classic," the young valet said, smiling.

"Thank you," she said as she handed him the keys. "We're just here for lunch, so won't be staying long."

"I'll keep your vehicle nearby," the valet replied. All his attention was on the classic Jeep rather than Dana or Courtney.

Courtney shrugged and said, "It seems like boys really love your jalopy."

"You'll come around to Big Red yet," Dana replied.

They made their way up the steps and walked inside, and as much as she disliked Gustavo Barca bankrolling Roy, and now Skylar's efforts to take Casa Verde away from her, she was the first to admit that Tranquil Bay was an exquisitely done hotel, and that was just from the lobby area.

"Okay, this is amazing," Dana said, looking around.

"I wasn't going to say anything, but wow, it's breathtaking," Courtney added.

From the porte cochère there were the grand steps, taking visitors up into a wide lobby with a high ceiling.

The lobby extended all the way to the back, and since the entire area was an open design, that allowed for breathtaking ocean views no matter where a person was standing in the lobby.

The check-in area and concierge desks were made from exotic cocobolo wood that Costa Rica was known for. The woods were polished bright and shiny in a kaleidoscope of hardwood colors that included shades of yellow, red, and brown.

"Welcome to the Tranquil Bay Resort, are you checking in?" An overeager front-desk person greeted Dana and Courtney with a wide smile.

"No. We're just here for lunch," Dana explained.

Dana was told how to make her way to the Tranquilo Restaurant.

They had to crisscross through the jungle-themed pool. It was one of those infinity pools that gave the optical illusion of dropping off the mountainside down into the Pacific Ocean. There were two swim-up bars and several Jacuzzis at its corners.

"I'm staying here tonight," Courtney said with a grin.

Dana shot her a dirty look.

"Too far?" Courtney said, laughing.

"Mmm-hmm," Dana said slowly.

"No wonder Britney Spears and the Kardashians stay here. It's so tony," Dana said, remembering the photographs she had seen of the celebrities staying at the resort.

The resort oozed swankiness with a modern construction that was open, and everywhere signs touted how green and environmentally friendly the resort was.

"This must be what they call eco-luxury," Dana said, scoffing about the new in-thing in luxury travel where the rich are pampered under the auspice that they were at the same time saving the planet in their thousand-dollar-a-night room.

"The more a company toots their horn about that, the less I believe it," Courtney said.

Dana nodded in agreement. "A multi-million dollar, two-hundred-room resort with luxury cabanas built in the middle of the jungle, yeah, that sounds very eco-friendly," she said, laughing.

Dana and Courtney had lunch at the causal poolside restaurant instead of the more fancy-looking restaurant inside the resort. The restaurant was called The Hamburger Shack. The only shack to it was its name.

A pretty young hostess with glowing olive skin, raven-black hair, and piercing brown eyes escorted Dana and Courtney to a table with a view of the pool.

A handsome waiter dressed in a short-sleeved white polo shirt and white shorts brought them glasses of cucumber water and menus.

Dana looked around the restaurant, and the whole staff was young and pretty.

"Only the young and the beautiful need apply," Dana whispered.

The two of them giggled. Dana picked up the menu and opened it.

"Farm-to-table, they're hitting all the popular buzzwords from back home," she said, studying the menu that was mostly geared towards American and European palates, definitely not the locals.

Dana ordered the California Burger, which was a burger with bacon and avocado that came with garlic fries, Courtney ordered fish and chips, and both ordered banana daiquiris to wash it all down.

The food was delicious. Dana had been expecting Barca to be a bottom-feeding cost-cutter serving barely edible food, but she had to give the devil his due. He knew how to build and run a world-class resort. But she wasn't about to let him bulldoze her out of Casa Verde.

After lunch, they meandered down to a beautiful courtyard

that led to a rock wall that overlooked Mariposa Beach. Beyond the wall was a well-maintained footpath that led down towards Dana's property and onto the town and its white sand beach.

The entrance to the footpath had two signs; one pointed towards the Private Beach, the other towards Town.

"I didn't think you could have private beaches in Costa Rica. Wasn't it all supposed to be open for public access?" Courtney asked.

"If anyone can figure out how to skirt the law so he can have a private beach at his resort, it would be Gustavo Barca," Dana said.

Dana figured once he had the land from his resort down into town, he would then try to buy out the town itself so he could annex it as part of his resort and then could tout to his wealthy guests that the resort down to Mariposa Beach was all their own private playground.

The plebs would be kept out. She got angry just thinking about it when someone came from behind.

"Excuse me, are you Miss Dana Kirkpatrick?"

Dana turned to see a young man in his twenties standing there, smiling.

He wore a resort uniform with a name tag that read Claudio, Assistant Manager, and like every other staff person she had seen so far, he was very good looking, with dark skin and brown eyes and hair. She figured he was one of Barca's goons there to kick her out.

"Yes, what's going on, Claudio?" Dana said, throwing him for a loop.

He giggled nervously and glanced down at his name tag.

"I was friends with your uncle," he said.

Her entire demeanor changed from fight mode to friendly acknowledgment.

"Oh, well, it's nice to meet you. I thought you were here to say that Gustavo Barca was kicking us out of the resort. How did you know it was me?"

"I saw the red Willys Jeep parked outside, and I asked the valet, who pointed you out from the lobby. Sorry for being so forward," Claudio said.

"It's okay. So, how did you know my uncle?"

"My parents worked for him," Claudio said, smiling.

"Oh, that's nice," Dana said, not catching on.

"They now work for you, I guess," he added.

Dana's eyebrows arched, and she gave him a puzzled look.

"My mom and dad work in Casa Verde. Ramón and Carmen Villalobos, perhaps you've met them already?" Claudio Villalobos said, smiling wide.

"Oh my gosh, it's so nice to meet you," Dana said, hugging Claudio. Courtney smiled wide.

Claudio explained how he grew up in Casa Verde and how Blake Kirkpatrick took a liking to the shy but hardworking go-getter who kept busy with his studies while helping his mom and dad with chores around Casa Verde.

Blake began to teach him English, and when young Claudio expressed an interest in working in hotel management, it was Blake who paid for his deep immersion English classes in Liberia and then encouraged and supported Claudio while he was a hotel management and tourism student at the University of Costa Rica's Liberia campus.

After graduation, he worked his way up from the front desk to concierge to supervisor at the Cariari Hotel in San José. Eager to get back to the Guanacaste Province, he jumped at the chance to go back home when the Tranquil Bay Resort opened.

After five years working there, he was now the Assistant Manager for the Concierge Services.

Dana was touched by what she heard that day. Her father always referred to her uncle Blake as Peter Pan. A hippie that never grew up. A naive do-gooder with a strong belief in Eastern philosophy, which for Dana's straight-laced father, his brother might as well have been dabbling in the occult.

But in front of her stood a young man that had benefited from her uncle's good deeds.

In supporting, encouraging, and mentoring Claudio, Uncle Blake ensured that the young man grew up and went to college, becoming the first member of his family to ever go to college and earn a degree.

It was too bad he was working for Barca's resort, but she understood why. It was a five-star luxury resort with a lot of excellent opportunities for a local boy done well.

"So, what are your goals, to become the General Manager someday?" Dana asked.

"For the last ten years, that's all I've ever wanted. Work my way up to General Manager for an international hotel like the Marriott or the Four Seasons so I could see the world. But the last two years, my ambition has changed. I see what this job and working for a man like Mr. Barca has done for the General Manager here and the way he treats his people. I can't be that way and I don't want to be like them. So I would like to open my own small hotel someday. Right down there in Mariposa Beach," Claudio said, pointing towards the sign marking the way to the beach town.

"I think that's a wonderful goal."

"My parents told me all about you. They really like you. My father says you remind him of Don Blake."

Before arriving at Mariposa Beach and moving into Casa Verde, Dana wouldn't have been sure how to take that statement, since all she heard from her parents was that her uncle was a no-good beach bum, but she was seeing there was a lot of good and kindness in Uncle Blake, and she took Claudio's comment as a compliment.

"I don't like to speak ill of the dead," Claudio said, making the sign of the cross, "but Mr. Roy Kirkpatrick was very different from his father. He had come to Casa Verde before Don Blake died and he treated it like a party zone. And his wife, she was even worse. They both made it very clear to my parents that once he inherited, he planned to sell the property or that he would keep it, tearing everything down, including their house, so he could build a bunch of condos that he could sell. She would tease my parents, making 'tic-toc' sounds and pointing at her wrist when Don Blake wasn't around. She warned them that their days of freeloading off of Don Blake would soon come to an end."

"Did they visit him often?"

"Not for a long time. It's my understanding that they had a falling-out and Don Blake was estranged from his son. Something that hurt him deep, but he didn't like the kind of man he had become since marrying Skylar," Claudio said.

"My uncle was adamant that your parents be taken care of under the same arrangements he had with them, and I'm planning to honor that."

Claudio smiled. "It's been very stressful these past few years with Don Blake sick and not knowing when Roy and Skylar would inherit the land and kick them out of their home. They were happily shocked when Mr. Campos explained to them that you had inherited the land, not Roy."

"You have had to deal with them staying here at the resort?"

"Unfortunately, yes. I don't think they remember me or know who I am, so I keep my mouth shut. But they've been staying here and driving the entire staff crazy. She's always complaining and telling everyone how much she hates Costa Rica. Going on and on about the heat, the mosquitoes, the food, and how she can't wait to get back to civilization."

"So why doesn't she just go?" Courtney asked.

"Money. The Casa Verde property is very valuable. I've heard about the big plans Mr. Barca has for this area once he takes over Casa Verde and a lot of the surrounding properties, too," Claudio said, leaning back against the short wall and looking towards the resort.

"Is Skylar here now?" Dana asked.

"She had been staying at one of the luxury cabanas with her husband, but just yesterday, Mr. Barca himself told her she had to leave the resort. He was going to put her up in one of his smaller rental properties in the town of Nosara," Claudio said.

That explained what Skylar was doing with Barca yesterday and why they seemed to be arguing.

"We ran into them in The Pueblo. They didn't see us, but they seemed to be arguing and they went into one of the offices there."

"That doesn't surprise me. As much as she complained about the resort, once Barca told her he was moving her out, she went crazy. The front desk supervisor and one of the security guards told me all about the brouhaha. She blew a gasket. Saying a lot of weird stuff, like...that she didn't care about the land and Casa Verde anymore and that if Mr. Barca kicked her out of the resort, she would just go back to California and he would lose the land," Claudio explained.

"So she stayed put?" Dana asked.

"No. Last I heard, she was given a firm but polite nudge out of the resort."

"When was that?" Dana asked.

"Yesterday."

"Claudio!" It was a whispered shout coming from another side of the pool. It was loud enough for them to hear it, yet low-key enough that the guests meandering around wouldn't notice it.

Claudio rolled his eyes.

"That's my boss. I need to go. Can you meet me at my parents' house tonight?"

"Yes, of course," Dana said.

"CLAUDIO!" This time the General Manager was full-on shouting and stomping his foot.

TWENTY-ONE

Later that evening, Benny joined Dana and Courtney at Casa Verde.

Dana told them about their jaunt up to the Tranquil Bay Resort.

Benny winced.

"Hey, even if Gustavo Barca wasn't Skylar's Daddy Moneybags, I still wanted to check out the resort in order to see if it lived up to the hype," she said.

"And we were hungry, we figured a five-star resort would have something good to eat," Courtney added in her two cents.

"So did it?" Benny asked incredulously.

"Unfortunately, yes. That no-good lout knows how to run a swanky resort," Dana said.

"The food was very good, but it came with U.S.—not Costa Rican—prices," Courtney said.

"Barca's target guests do not fret about the price of a meal. He has it down to a science. His staff meets arriving guests at the Liberia airport and they are ferried over to the resort in posh, air-conditioned, Wi-Fi-enabled Mercedes Benz shuttle buses. The driver is under strict orders not to stop until they arrive at the resort. Barca has everything arranged to keep the guests at the resort during their whole stay in Costa Rica. Any off-site activity is coordinated by the resort's concierge staff, some of the best in the business, who make sure any off-site location is either owned by Barca, his partners, or it's a location that offers a nice kickback to Barca's company for each busload of tourists sent their way. The businesses here in town do not see any of that money. The resort discourages guests from venturing down here by scaring them into believing this is a dangerous town full of shady expats, drug kingpins, and untrusting locals. The only resort tourists that make it down to town are the more adventure-seeking types that are suffering from resort fever and who don't fall for the resort's boogeyman tales about our little community," Benny explained.

"That's awful," Dana said.

"Gustavo Barca has not been a good neighbor, which makes it such a gall that he comes down here to eat at Ike's restaurant or to buy dozens of Mindy's bagels and homemade cream cheese," Benny said.

"It's interesting that you mentioned the concierge staff," Dana said, eyes wide.

"Did they arrange a surfing lesson for you?" Benny asked mockingly.

"Funny guy, no, we have Big Mike for that, but do you have any plans tonight at eight p.m.?"

Benny gave her a curious look.

Dana told him about meeting Claudio Villalobos, the concierge services assistant manager and son of Ramón and Carmen.

"I know Claudio well. He's a wonderful young man."

Courtney took a nap while Dana finished reading her book. Benny was on his laptop until it was time to meet with Claudio.

Dana, Courtney, and Benny made the quick walk from

Casa Verde down to Ramón and Carmen's house. It was a lovely home. Dana could see their house from her wraparound porch and from her second-floor deck. She tried not to gawk down at their house, wanting to give them their privacy. So she was excited to finally visit the house.

She noticed, for the first time, a nicely built chicken coop off to one side. Dana had noticed the chickens running around the property. Ramón had asked if it was okay, and Dana was more than thrilled, hoping for some free-range chicken eggs from time to time.

The hen house was fenced in with a nice long run and a heavy-duty galvanized wire to protect the chickens from their long list of predators: feral cats, dogs, raccoons, skunks, coyotes, foxes, humans. Seemed just about every creature preyed on the poor, hapless chickens.

She had yet to knock on the door when it opened and Ramón stood there, smiling,

"Please come in," he said.

Carmen came out of the kitchen, also smiling. Claudio was sitting on the couch, watching television. He shut it off and stood up to greet the guests.

They sat around the dining room table. Carmen brought out coffee, milk, and galletas de mantequilla, butter cookies from Costa Rican Pozuelo Cookie Company.

The cookies looked delicious, but eating them and drinking strong coffee after eight o'clock at night wasn't something Dana's body was accustomed to, but *when in Rome*, she thought as she poured herself half a cup of coffee, filled the rest of the cup with the warm milk, and grabbed one of the cookies.

"That Skylar is a big pain in the rear," Claudio said, quickly adding, "Sorry, no offense."

"Believe me, none taken. We were never close, and she's

been a big pain in my behind for months now," Dana said, taking a bite of the butter cookie. Her eyes narrowed in approval.

"You had asked about Roy and Skylar. They stayed at the resort for months. They arrived during the rainy season, or as we call it in the resort business, the slow season. At first, Mr. Barca put them up in one of the exquisite suites by the pool, not that it impressed Skylar, who complained about the pool noise, the AC not cooling down the place enough to her liking, and that it was too noisy, and on and on. Mr. Barca got tired of her complaints, so he had them moved down to one of the less desirable jungle bungalows, the one furthest from the main resort area. It was still beautiful, but not as nice as the suites. Not surprisingly, she complained even worse about the new lodging. She demanded to be back in the main area of the resort. She was rude and nasty to staff, guests, everyone, including Mr. Barca. The lion's share of the abuse was reserved for her husband. He was no picnic, but next to her, he was a saint," Claudio said.

"Those are the bungalows by the footpath going from the resort to Mariposa Beach?" Benny asked.

"Yes. They're very nice. Mr. Barca doesn't build anything for his resort that isn't top-notch and luxurious. No dumps. Well, except for the staff quarters. Those are a dump. Mr. Barca is the face of five-star luxury for his hotels and his upscale gated communities, and at the same time, he's a slumlord for the housing projects he puts up for his staff," Claudio said.

"I've heard about that. He does a good job of keeping that side of his business quiet," Benny said.

"Well, he couldn't keep Doña Skylar quiet. She was always complaining about this and that and berating people. It wasn't surprising to the staff that Don Roy began to spend more and more time away from the resort. I would get all the gossip from my staff. Supposedly, Roy had become enlightened by a yogi lady in Nosara, if you catch my drift," Claudio said, blushing.

"You don't say," Dana said, leaning forward.

"Well, it was just gossip, until I personally heard them fight about it. My boss stuck me with trying to appease those two, since they demanded to deal with management, not staff. It has been the most challenging assignment of my career so far," Claudio said, shaking his head.

"Anyway. One night, they sent me down to check on them, since there were noise complaints. I got outside of their bungalow when I heard them fighting. I know I shouldn't have, but I eavesdropped. She was going on about how humiliated she was that he was spending so much time away. It made her look like a fool. And that they needed to focus on the case so they could sell Casa Verde so she could go back to civilization. But it seemed he was wavering on that. He finally had enough of her abuse, so he stormed off and she yelled, 'Go ahead, run to your little yoga tramp,' and he just left, cursing. I heard glassware breaking. It wasn't the first time she threw a glass or plate against the wall in anger," Claudio said.

"What did you do?" Dana asked.

"Roy didn't see me when he left, and after she broke a few dishes, she quieted down, so I just quietly left. I don't like dealing with her when she's not angry, but under those circumstances, I just wanted to run away."

"So she never saw you that night?" Dana asked.

"No. Well, I don't think so. I'm sure I would have heard her scream at me had she seen me," Claudio replied.

"When did this all happen?"

"The same night of Roy's murder."

Dana, Courtney, and Benny exchanged Joe Friday-Bill Gannon nods with each other.

"Correct me if I'm wrong, Claudio, but aren't those bunga-lows near where Roy's body was found?" Benny asked.

"Yes, that is why I assume she killed him. The entire resort staff thinks Skylar killed Roy. There is a pool going on, I believe it's up to five thousand colones," Claudio said, matter-of-factly.

"I don't know," Courtney said. "She's crazy and all, but to kill her own husband? Does she really have that inside of her?"

"We all have that inside of us," Benny said.

Dana furrowed her brow at Benny. "Remind me not to tick you off," she said.

Claudio smiled.

"So maybe the killing doesn't have anything to do with the land, but a jealous wife. That should be enough of a motive for the police to take another good look at Skylar," Dana said.

"According to Picado, Skylar has an ironclad alibi," Benny said.

"The alibi is from Mr. Barca," Claudio said.

That stunned Dana and Benny. "I know because I was told to corroborate it if the detectives asked me. I was supposed to say that she was at the resort the whole time and that she had been seen the night of the murder at the bar. But that's not true. I don't know if she left her bungalow or not, but she wasn't at the bar when Roy was killed and no one saw her there, that I do know," Claudio said.

"Have you told Detective Picado about all this?" Dana asked.

Claudio looked away in shame. "No. Mr. Barca said that if any of us talks to anyone about the goings-on inside the resort, including the police, that they would be fired, and he would blacklist us so we could never get another job at a resort. That we would be lucky to find a job managing a Burger King," Claudio said.

"So why are you telling us?" Dana asked.

"Like I told you at the resort. My parents like you, and I owe a lot to your uncle Blake. Mr. Barca wants to expand his resort and add a posh gated community for the rich by buying up all the land near it. This includes your land, Doña Dana. He'll bulldoze Casa Verde and my parents' home, and that yoga retreat, and that farm near the resort, that's where my ninety-nine-year-old great-grandmother and my grandparents live. Barca will relocate them into a state-run old people's home. Those plans were bad enough, but now covering up a murder? I can't go along with any of that," Claudio said, his voice inflecting upward.

Dana and Courtney looked at each other, dumbfounded.

"Jeez, Dana, what have you gotten yourself into?" Courtney asked.

"I get that Gustavo Barca is a greedy developer, that seems to be par for the course in that business, but can he really be that nasty and downright evil?" Dana asked.

"He has a one-track mind to expand his empire. And there have always been rumors about the things he did in Venezuela to make his fortune before falling out of favor with the Chavista government in Caracas, so it wouldn't surprise me that he would be that ruthless and that he would protect a murderer so he could get his hands on Casa Verde," Benny said.

"We need to tell Detective Picado about all this," Courtney said.

"Picado will have a conniption if he finds out we're meddling. He is convinced that Skylar wasn't involved in killing Roy. If you go challenging him on that, he'll go loco on you," Benny warned.

"He might not know about this yoga teacher, and he doesn't know the alibi is a fake," Dana said.

"But he knows about the divorce filings in the States, so he knows that Roy and Skylar didn't exactly have a happy marriage," Benny said.

"Most marriages aren't happy," Dana said, sounding bitter as she thought about the demise of her own marriage.

Embarrassed, she turned to face Claudio and asked, "Do you know who this yoga teacher is?"

Claudio nodded that he did.

"Great, I want to meet her."

TWENTY-TWO

Against Benny's objections, Dana made plans to go up to Nosara in the morning to talk to Roy's yoga teacher. If she could confirm that Roy had been romantically involved with her, then that information, along with Claudio agreeing to share what he had overheard go down between Skylar and Roy, might be enough for the detective to take another look at Skylar.

According to Claudio, the yoga teacher's name was Marisol Arias; she taught classes at Yoga Trópico, a popular yoga studio in Nosara Beach.

Claudio had reiterated that he didn't know if the rumors were true, but Dana decided it was something she had to find out for herself, so she could present Picado with facts, not rumors. It was looking more to Dana that Roy's murder was not about Casa Verde but because of a love triangle, and that Skylar was the killer.

"If that's true, Skylar is pretty brazen to stay in the country once they cleared her. Especially since she has a nice life insurance payout coming her way now that the police have cleared her as a suspect. I would hightail it out of here," Benny said.

"Skylar has always been greedy. She's not going to walk away from a potential windfall from selling Casa Verde to Barca," Dana said.

Benny had tagged along with Dana and Courtney up to Nosara. She felt excited that he was coming along.

"For legal advice," Dana said to Courtney after she grinned a bit too wide for Dana's comfort.

"Uh-huh, his legal advice is to not go find this yoga teacher, so it's not like you follow his legal advice anyway," Courtney said, grinning.

Dana smiled. *Busted.* "But I appreciate it, no matter if I don't accept it."

"Whatever, I know why you're excited."

Dana rolled her eyes and ignored her.

On their way to Benny's beach house, they stopped at Mindy's for coffee and bagels.

"I'll watch Big Red," Courtney said, yawning.

Dana smiled. She needed coffee to get going in the morning, but Courtney needed it to function.

Mindy greeted Dana warmly. It was the third straight morning she was there.

"You're becoming one of my regulars. I love it," Mindy said.

Dana smiled and ordered three large coffees, two lox bagels, one for her, one for Benny, and an egg and bacon sesame bagel for Courtney.

"Coming right up," Mindy said, her face turning dark. "Ugh, Mr. Sunshine is here," Mindy said, nodding towards the window. Dana turned to see Detective Picado getting out of his unmarked car. "I get it. He sees a lot of bad stuff in his line of work, but he's so ornery, that one," Mindy said, disappearing to the back.

Dana tensed up. She wanted to follow Mindy to the back of

the coffee shop and hide. But she breathed in deeply. *Stay calm*, she said to herself.

Picado walked in and beelined towards Dana.

"I thought that was your Jeep out there," he said without saying hello.

"Yes, it is." She was able to muster half a smile.

"It's very distinctive, that vehicle, which is why when it was brought to my attention that that there was an American woman in a red Willys Jeep bothering people at the Tranquil Bay Resort, I knew they were talking about you," Picado said, shooting Dana an icy stare.

Dana was aghast, and she couldn't hide it from her face.

Then she got angry. She was sick and tired of being needled by the detective. She was sick and tired of being afraid of him. She didn't care that she was in a foreign country and that he considered her a suspect. She was in Costa Rica to make her home, and she didn't care about preventive detention anymore. The threat he lorded over her like a dirty gym sock. Detective or not, he was a bully, and she hated bullies. *To heck with him*, she thought.

"Excuse me? I bothered no one. I can go to the resort if I want and talk to whoever I want. Besides, I wanted to have lunch there and check out that fancy hotel everyone talks about. Is there a law against that?" *Don't get too angry, Dana, calm your nerves so you don't just sound like a crazy person*, she reminded herself before continuing to speak without letting him reply.

"Who said I was bothering them? I spoke to the valet that parked my car, the waiter, and two staff people, that was it. So who complained? Was there a formal complaint levied against me?"

Picado's brow furrowed. She could tell he was taken aback by her aggressive rapid-fire questions and her newfound moxie.

Picado cleared his throat. "Well, I'm not at liberty—"

She interrupted him, "So there isn't an official complaint, you're not charging me with bothering anyone at the resort, or are you?"

"No," he said.

"Are you any closer to finding out who killed my cousin, or are you too busy with resort business?" Dana said. *Don't go too far*, she reminded herself.

A muffled laugh came from behind the counter as Mindy tried, in vain, to stifle it.

Picado glared at Mindy.

"Here's your order, hon," Mindy said, breaking the tension.

Dana turned around to look at Mindy. "Thank you, how much do I owe you?"

"Today's breakfast is on the house, darling," Mindy said, smiling widely.

"Thank you so much, you're so sweet," Dana replied. Both women ignored Picado, who was stewing behind Dana.

Dana turned to face him with her order in her hands. "I have to go," she said to Picado.

"I'm warning you again, stop interfering in my case," Picado said as he stormed out of the coffee shop.

Once he left, Dana turned to Mindy, and she felt shaky.

"I can't believe I did that."

"You were great," Mindy said, reaching over the counter to hug Dana.

With the anger-fueled adrenaline boost gone, she shivered like she was in Siberia in the winter, not in tropical Costa Rica. But she felt empowered, and ready to get to the bottom of her cousin's murder and to nip in the bud the property dispute with Skylar once and for all so she could move on with her new life. And her standing up to Picado got her free coffee and bagels to boot.

A good start to the day, she thought as she walked out towards Big Red feeling ten feet taller. Courtney was still sitting there, looking groggy.

TWENTY-THREE

Benny's place was about a ten-minute drive from Mindy's coffee and bagel shop.

It was the first time she was visiting his beach house, since he always came over to Casa Verde, so she was excited to see what it looked like.

Dana drove as Courtney struggled to keep the coffee from flying out of its to-go cups with each crater-sized pothole that Big Red encountered.

Dana told her about her little altercation with Picado.

"I'm glad you stood up for yourself, but I really think you're playing with fire with him."

"I have done nothing wrong, so I'm not letting him or Barca push me around. I can always write an exposé about those two when I'm done dealing with this," Dana said.

Courtney looked at her nervously. She was nervous for her friend and nervous that the next pothole would toss the contents of the three cups of piping-hot coffee on her lap.

"I get it, they didn't make cup holders back in the forties, but when your uncle refurbished and modernized this jalopy, why didn't he put in some cup holders?" Courtney said, changing the subject.

They both laughed as Dana maneuvered around a pothole as Big Red dipped down to its right side.

"Oh, sheesh, can you try to miss some of those potholes? You're like ten for ten," Courtney said teasingly.

Dana looked in the rearview mirror and then glanced at the side mirror. "I think that was a sinkhole, not a pothole."

They both continued to laugh, driving the wild roads of rural Costa Rica.

Dana pulled into Benny's house, which was in the outskirts of town. It was a two-story house, painted white. Benny's house style and amenities were very similar to Casa Verde, but the house hadn't been remodeled or touched much since Benny's father first built it in the early 1980s. Dana thought it was a lovely home, but she appreciated the amount of work that her Uncle Blake had put into modernizing Casa Verde.

Benny welcomed Dana and Courtney at the door.

"You dressed the part," Benny said, smiling. Dana had dressed up in yoga gear.

"Might as well try to get her to identify with me through yoga."

Benny gave Dana and Courtney a quick tour of the three-bedroom house. Dana blushed at lingering too long at his bedroom. She didn't know why she was so curious to see where he slept, but Courtney noticed and smiled. Dana shook her off with pursed lips.

After the tour, they sat out on the front patio and ate their bagels and drank the coffee that Courtney had valiantly saved from the jeep-eating potholes.

Dana had decided not to tell Benny about her confrontation with Detective Picado and pinky-swore Courtney to not say anything about it, either.

She wasn't sure why she didn't want him to know. She just felt that was something she needed to handle on her own without having Benny worry about it or wanting to interfere.

After eating the bagels and drinking the coffee, they piled into Benny's Land Cruiser, leaving Big Red at his house, and they headed up to Nosara on Dana's little mission to talk to the yoga teacher that might have stolen Roy's heart, much to Skylar's anger.

Benny and Courtney thought Dana was being too reckless and that she should stay in Casa Verde under self-imposed house arrest, but doing nothing was like asking Takeru Kobayashi to not eat too many hot dogs.

"I need to get back to San José for a few days. I need to do some work on your case, and I have two closings for other clients I need to attend," Benny said, driving.

Dana blinked a few times, looking out the window. It was as if she had forgotten that she was Benny's client and that he didn't live in Mariposa Beach year-round.

They had spent so much time together since she arrived in town that it felt like their relationship had become more than that. *There you go, building things up in your head*, Dana chastised herself.

"When are you leaving?"

"Tomorrow," Benny said, sadness in his voice. Or maybe that was just in Dana's head.

She nodded.

"But I'll be right back as soon as I can. A few days," Benny added quickly.

Dana felt her heart skip a beat in excitement.

She turned and smiled at Benny. "That's great, you've been so kind and helpful," Dana said, her voice trailing off then quickly adding, "to me and Courtney."

Dana glanced over at Courtney, who sat in the backseat quietly with a huge grin on her face.

Yoga Trópico was on the second floor of a two-story building in Nosara Beach, which was about fifteen minutes from the main town of Nosara—where the airport and El Pueblo were located and where Dana and Courtney had seen Gustavo Barca and Skylar arguing.

Nosara Beach looked similar to Mariposa Beach—a bit larger, more shops, more people, bigger waves, and a lot of yogis stuff.

Benny parked in front of the building.

"We can't all three go up there to ambush her, it will freak her out. So I'll go up there to see her," Dana said.

Dana could tell by the look on their faces that Benny and Courtney wanted to disagree, but they knew she was right.

"Be careful. For all we know, you're going up there to confront Roy's killer," Benny said.

His comment took her aback. She hadn't thought perhaps she had been the one that killed Roy.

"She a yoga teacher," Dana said, sounding incredulous.

"She's human. All signs point to her having an affair with Roy. Love triangles make people do crazy things to other people. So just as Skylar is one corner of the triangle that might have snapped into killing Roy, we could say the same about this yoga teacher. I don't care how enlightened she is. Be careful."

The more she mulled it over, the more it made sense to her. She had been on a one-track mind that Skylar killed Roy, but perhaps it was the other woman in the relationship that killed him.

TWENTY-FOUR

Dana had checked Marisol's schedule online, so she knew the yoga teacher would be in-between classes for a couple hours.

She waited for her by the stairs at the bottom floor of the building that housed the yoga studio.

She could hear yoga mantras coming from upstairs, which meant they were wrapping up.

Five minutes later, sweaty-looking men and women with rolled-up yoga mats started to come down the stairs in droves. *Class must be over*, Dana thought.

Dana recalled what she had learned about the yoga teacher from her website. Marisol Arias was twenty-seven-years-old. She had raven-black hair in a pixie cut. She was a tica from a well-to-do family, as most Western yogis seemed to be. Marisol had grown up in Cartago, which was the third largest city in Costa Rica, located less than twenty miles from the capital of San José.

She had come to Nosara four years ago to take classes to become a yoga teacher and had stayed on because business was good in Nosara for yoga teachers, where American and European tourists came for beach, sun, surf, and yoga.

Dana's mind raced as she had an argument with herself: *I feel like a stalker. You are a stalker. Lurking down here, waiting for her. I'm not lurking, just waiting.*

Ten minutes later, Marisol Arias came down the stairs. She looked just as pretty in person as she did on the yoga studio's website. Dana thought there was sadness behind her big, bright green eyes.

"Hi, Marisol," Dana said.

Marisol had no clue who Dana was, but she looked at the Lululemon-clad American and smiled. "Hi, were you at my class?"

"No. But I was hoping to talk to you for just a moment. Can I buy you a cup of coffee?" Dana asked.

Marisol's brow furrowed, her face turning from friendly to casting a suspicious look at Dana.

"What about?"

"I'm Roy Kirkpatrick's cousin, Dana Kirkpatrick."

Tears welled up in Marisol's eyes.

They walked down the block to a small coffee shop that shared space with a bakery. Marisol ordered a green tea and pineapple empanada. Dana ordered a latte and a scone. They sat at a round table for two outside on the sidewalk, facing a street lined with palm trees, and although Dana couldn't see the ocean from there, she could hear it.

"So you're his cousin from San Francisco, the one who inherited Casa Verde," Marisol said, tearing off a piece of her pastry and putting it in her mouth. She was studying her closely.

"That's me. I take it Roy talked to you about me."

"Oh, yes," Marisol said.

"Probably not all good, huh?"

"It upset him about the inheritance, but it was mostly resentment that his father cared for you more than him."

"I don't know about that. I don't think it was that clear-cut," Dana said.

"In Roy's mind, the fact that his father left you that property instead of him meant just that. It was clear-cut to him," Marisol replied.

"I have no idea what caused Uncle Blake to do what he did, but that is what he wanted."

"It's not what Roy wanted. But it seemed most everything in Roy's life was not what he wanted," Marisol said, tears streaming down her cheeks. She quickly dabbed at them with her yoga hand sleeve.

"You sound like you talked to him a lot...about personal stuff...more than a regular yoga teacher would have talked to a student," Dana said, trying to broach on the subject.

Marisol looked away and took another bite of the empanada, then sipped more tea. She said nothing, so Dana figured the gentle broaching wasn't working and decided to not beat around the bush. "Were you having an affair with Roy?"

Marisol almost spit out her tea. "I can tell you're related to Roy," she said.

"We Kirkpatricks are known for being a bit direct and blunt," Dana said, smiling.

"It's a good trait to have. The more you bottle things inside, the more it tears you apart. I'm an expert at that," Marisol said.

Dana watched her as she put her cup of tea down and looked around. It was as if she was trying to center herself to gather the strength to speak her true self.

"I liked that in Roy. I like honesty, which is why it was so hard to have been so dishonest with my true relationship with Roy. The short answer to your question is yes. But it wasn't something cheap or tawdry. It was not a fling. We had something special. And I know people scoff and are cynical about finding one's soul mate, but I believe in that, and I had finally found my soul mate in Roy," Marisol said, more tears trickling down her cheeks. "He was a wonderful gentleman." Now it was Dana that almost spit out her latte.

Dana hadn't seen the good parts of Roy in so long that she forgot they were there, buried deep, and perhaps Marisol was able to bring them back up to the surface. Turn that lump of black charcoal into a bright diamond.

"We've had our issues, but it's nice to hear that," Dana said, and she found that she meant it.

"Now I've lost him in this life," Marisol said, wiping away tears.

"I'm sorry to upset you," Dana said.

Marisol let out a sound that was part cry and laugh. It sounded like relief to Dana. Like she could finally talk about the loss she felt.

"Don't be sorry. It feels good to share this with someone else. I've never gotten involved with a married man before. But he came to my class and I could tell there was so much bitterness and sadness to Roy and that there was a decent man inside wanting to be let out, but all he had known for most of his adult life was the toxicity from his relationships, the estrangement with his father, an unhappy marriage, countless business failures—that's what twisted Roy into being hard and mean," Marisol said, looking at her hands on the table. She then looked up to Dana and laughed. "I must sound like a naïve, crazy fool to you," she said, looking away.

Dana shook her head. "Far from it. You make me feel happy. I knew that other Roy before life and Skylar embittered him. It makes me happy to know that you had brought that out in him before he died."

"He told me about you. He always liked you—said you two were close when you were growing up but then just drifted apart and stopped having much of a familial relationship."

"That's true. Our relationship in the last decade amounted to a few Facebook likes here and there. Then when his father died and left me Casa Verde, well, he was so angry with me, and I understood why he was mad. And I'd like to believe that we could have resolved this amicably if it wasn't for Skylar fueling his rage," Dana said.

"I think that's true. There are some people who don't know how to feel anything inside but anger, outrage, hatred, and so they waste their life going from one dispute to another so it becomes the norm for them. A life without drama to a person like Skylar is like not living."

Dana nodded in agreement. "You're very insightful. I can see why Roy liked you," Dana said.

"Loved," Marisol corrected Dana. "We were only together for two months and we had to keep it secret, but we were in love. And it wasn't an infatuation, it was a real love," Marisol said, her voice wavering.

"I'm glad to hear he had found happiness. I'm trying to find out who killed him," Dana said.

"I know who killed him. It was that woman," Marisol said.

"Skylar?" Dana asked.

"Yes, HER. You see..." Marisol took a moment and breathed in and out before continuing to speak. "Roy was changing, and she hated it. The good that was in him from the start was coming out. He no longer wanted to hide our love. Neither of us wanted to do that anymore. So he was going to leave Skylar, for good this time. Stay here with me for a while or maybe we would move to San José or to the States. But we wanted to start our life together. And he was going to put the legal dispute with you behind him. He didn't care about Casa Verde anymore as long as we were together. He knew it would all work out without lawyers fighting like dogs over a bone."

Dana found that hard to fathom. She thought back on the

last time she saw him when he and Skylar confronted her. He still seemed hurt about his father giving her the property. But he seemed conflicted. It was Skylar that was being the belligerent one. Even if he wanted to change course and be civil, Skylar jumped in to stoke the resentment he had still burning inside of him.

"He told you this? He said he was leaving Skylar and wanted to settle the property dispute with me?"

"Yes. He told me that more than once. And then he said he was going to tell Skylar the truth about everything and that he was leaving her that very weekend, but by Sunday night, he was dead."

TWENTY-FIVE

Dana and Marisol spent about a heart-wrenching hour at the coffee shop, talking. Benny had planted the seed that she might be Roy's killer, but after meeting and talking with her, Dana knew that wasn't the case.

Dana walked back to the Land Cruiser, where Benny and Courtney were waiting. She climbed inside. It was chilly inside, since Benny had kept the car running to keep the AC going.

Dana sighed. "That was sad and happy rolled into one." She saw Courtney and Benny exchange puzzled looks.

"How was she?" Courtney asked.

"She was nice. And she was having an affair with Roy." Dana said it so nonchalantly.

"Really? She admitted it?"

"It was a relief. But it was more than an affair. They were in love. Soul mates, she said."

Courtney scoffed. "They just met."

"It's been known to happen that fast," Benny said.

Courtney smiled and looked at Dana. Benny blushed.

"It's the granizado vendor," he said, changing the subject.

"Huh?"

"Snow cones, the Costa Rica way. Delicious," Benny said, jumping out of the car and heading towards an old man pushing what looked like to Dana was an ice cream cart.

"I guess you can tell us more about the soul mates after snow cones," Courtney said, exiting the truck. Dana followed suit.

It was hot and humid, another day in the tropics. The granizado vendor was making his way towards a park where Benny sat on the bench.

"It's like an oven here," Courtney complained.

"I thought you Californians would be used to this weather," Benny teased.

"I was born and raised in Michigan and I've lived in foggy-cool San Francisco for ten years. I'm not used to this heat," Courtney said, using her hand like a fan.

Dana laughed. She sat on the bench. It was hot. She looked down at her flip-flops, convinced even her toes were on fire.

The old man pushing the cart finally reached them and asked them if they wanted granizados.

"Ah, just what the doctor ordered," Benny said, rubbing his hands.

"What are graw-nee-saw-dos," Courtney asked, butchering the Spanish.

"Basically, it's delicious sugary syrup poured on top of shaved ice," Benny explained.

"You had me at sugar and ice," Dana said from the bench.

Benny ordered three granizados. Dana watched the old man with his wide smile. He was missing a few teeth. He seemed happy to make the sale. He opened what looked like an ice cream cart as a cool mist from the ice inside billowed outward. Dana got up from the bench to look inside. There were huge blocks of ice in the cart. Courtney stood next to her, peeking inside too.

"Oh, that feels nice. It's like opening up the freezer on a hot day," she said.

The old man said with a laugh, "Muy frío," very cold in Spanish.

"Se siente rico," *feels good*, Dana said to the old man.

He grabbed what looked like an ice scraper with a scoop attached to it and he began to grate it over a huge block of ice as he scooped the shaved ice into a white cone cup.

"Qué sabor se les ofrece?" *What flavor would you like*, the old man asked, pointing at several bottles on his cart.

"That's the syrup?" Courtney asked.

"Yes. Which flavor do you want?" Benny asked.

"What are the flavors?"

"Red, blue, green, orange, and purple," Benny said, smiling.

"Can't go wrong with purple, I guess."

"Red for me," Dana said.

Benny relayed that to the old man, who grabbed a large bottle and began to drizzle the syrup onto the ice like a hot dog vendor pouring mustard on a dog. He then picked up a can of condensed milk and drizzled it on the cone. He handed the cone to Courtney and repeated the process on the second cone, which he handed over to Benny.

Dana tasted it and smiled. The old man smiled back, knowing from her look that he had a happy customer.

Benny paid the old man, who thanked him and then went back on his way pushing his cart down towards the beach to provide the icy treats to the sun-kissed tourists.

"He's adorable," Dana said as the old man continued on his way, shouting out "granizados" every few steps.

"And these are delicious snow cones," Courtney added.

"Some vendors get really elaborate in their granizado making, pouring not just syrup and condensed milk but also powdered milk and topping it off with pineapple chunks. There is also the Churchill. I'll have to take you guys to get a Churchill," Benny said, sounding excited.

"What's a Churchill?"

"It's the granddaddy of all granizados in Costa Rica."

Suddenly, Benny said, "Oh, great." He was being facetious as he looked at a white car parked across the park.

"Is that who I think it is?" Dana asked.

"It's Detective Picado," Benny replied.

"He hasn't seen us."

Picado stayed in the car as Detective Gabriela Rojas exited it and went inside the building. A couple minutes later, she came back downstairs and went back inside the car.

"He must have found out about the yoga teacher and is now looking to interview her."

A couple minutes later, Marisol Arias was walking back to the yoga studio.

Picado and Rojas exited the car, waiting for her, when he looked over towards the park, and Dana and Picado locked eyes.

If looks could kill, she would be dead.

He crossed the street and walked towards them.

"Ms. Kirkpatrick, what are you doing with Ms. Arias?" Picado demanded to know.

"I just met her today. We had tea and coffee."

"Unbelievable. Everyone is here. A nice little party you are all having," Picado said, glaring at the three of them and then at Marisol Arias, whom Detective Rojas had brought over to join the powwow.

"What are we doing wrong?" Dana asked.

"You're interfering with my investigation," Picado barked loudly.

Benny and Courtney arrived and stood next to Dana so they were all facing the detectives.

"You're all interfering with my investigation. I should arrest all of you for obstruction of justice," Picado said, eyeballing everyone.

"What obstruction?" Dana asked, trying hard to contain her anger.

Benny gently put his hand on her arm and he stepped in front of Dana and Picado.

"My client just wanted to meet Ms. Arias, that's all, we had no idea we couldn't talk to people in town."

"How was I supposed to know about your investigation? It's not like you're sending me updates. I found out about Marisol and Roy and I wanted to meet her. We had a lovely chat, and that's it," Dana said.

Benny once again gently touched her right arm. Courtney pinched her and whispered, "Preventive detention."

Dana got the hints, so she stayed quiet as Picado chastised them more for getting in the way of his investigation. After more jail threats and warnings to stop interfering, Picado was done beating his chest. He ordered Rojas to take Marisol back up to the yoga studio and wait for him there so he could conduct his interview.

Marisol looked terrified.

Dana nodded at her and mouthed *sorry*.

"If you find out about anyone else that might have information about this case, you call me and tell me about them, you don't go to them directly unless I say it's okay, is that clear?" Picado said. He had removed his jacket. Perhaps it was getting too hot—it was the tropics after all—but Dana thought it was more about showing them his pistol, handcuffs, and badge, all clipped to his belt.

"Okay," Dana said.

"No problem, Detective, thank you," Benny said, trying to be more contrite, then he quickly turned to Dana and Courtney and said, "Let's go, now."

They crossed the street and piled into the Land Cruiser as Benny drove away.

"That was intense," he said as he drove back towards Mariposa Beach.

Dana noticed he wasn't being as careful about missing the potholes as he had been on the way up, in a rush to get out of dodge and away from Picado.

"He couldn't really hold us in jail, could he?" Dana said.

"Preventive detention, Dana," Courtney yelped from the backseat.

"He's a cop. He can do anything he wants. Now, it might not stick, but that doesn't mean he couldn't have thrown us into the system for a few hours just to teach us a lesson. I wouldn't want to spend a minute locked up in their holding cells," Benny said.

"Well, he's a jerk," Dana said.

"I doubt even his own mother would argue that he isn't, but try to see it from his perspective: he's investigating a murder, and just at about every turn he runs into you, who, I remind you, might very well still be at the top of his suspect list."

Dana then told Courtney and Benny all about Roy and his soul mate yogi and how there was no way Marisol was the killer.

"It had to be Skylar," Dana said.

"So you think Skylar killed Roy because he was cheating on her? Those two have been splitting up and divorcing for years, why would she snap now?" Courtney asked.

"It's one thing to say I want a divorce because we've grown apart or all we do is fight, or something like that, but to tell Skylar he wants a divorce so he can be with his much younger, prettier, yoga teacher with that fit little body of hers...well, that's a bit different of a pill to swallow, and I'm talking from my own divorce experience," Dana said.

"And Barca kicks her out of the resort to live in a ho-hum apartment in town, adding insult to injury."

"Toss in the life insurance and Casa Verde with a buyer all lined up who is also supporting them financially in Costa Rica. If Roy divorces Skylar, that makes that deal a lot more complicated with Skylar left standing alone in a round of musical chairs," Benny said.

"I was thinking. Barca is a ruthless businessman. Roy and Skylar splitting up and Roy dropping his lawsuit against me, well, that would throw a monkey wrench into Barca's plans just as bad as to Skylar's dreams for a big payday and free lodging. He has a lot of money invested into Roy and Skylar waiting for the payoff, which seems to be slipping from his grasp. Maybe he got tired of dealing with the Roy and Skylar drama and now he has a love triangle to contend with, so he figures he's better off dealing with Skylar alone instead of lovesick Roy and his new girlfriend," Dana said.

"You really think a rich guy like that would kill someone?" Courtney asked, not sounding convinced.

"How difficult would it be for a powerful man like Gustavo Barca to have someone killed?" Dana asked.

"I'm afraid it wouldn't be too difficult," Benny replied.

That shook Dana up. "And if he then uses that power to point the finger at me for the murder, he gets two birds with one stone. It's all over. It's Yahtzee for me."

TWENTY-SIX

There was an odd feeling in the air, and it wasn't from the sweltering heat and humidity. Dana felt like she had been charged, tried, and convicted of the crime of murder but had been allowed to remain free for a few days to get her affairs in order. At least that's the urgency she felt about finding out if Skylar or Gustavo Barca had killed Roy.

She felt like a pariah in town and she had barely been there for a week. *Some fresh start,* she thought.

Dana could feel eyes on her from the community and even from the tourists who would have a little something extra to talk about with their trip to Costa Rica when they got back home.

Mindy was the exception. Her coffee shop and bagel joint had become part of Dana's daily routine.

Mindy's husband, Leo, had become more standoffish when Dana came to the coffee shop. He was pleasant and polite and he greeted her with a smile, but it was a worrisome smile that couldn't hide him not wanting Dana coming around every day and becoming friends with his wife when she might be a cold-blooded killer. Dana didn't blame him for having those thoughts. He didn't know her from Adam, and he worried about his wife's well-being.

Mindy had told her that she remembered what it was like being the latest foreign expat living in a new country and moving down to a small, tight-knit community like Mariposa Beach, making things even tougher for a new expat.

The locals and the longtime expats both look down on the new arrivals with suspicion and derision, and that was just from moving into town. Toss in being a single, newly divorced woman, and that tipped the scale even more against an expat lasting too long. Add to that the property dispute and chatter about Dana selfishly keeping Casa Verde instead of letting the son of Blake Kirkpatrick get the property—even if doing that was going against the beloved former resident's final will and testament.

And to add to the pile of manure that had stacked high against Dana, there was the gossip that Picado was looking into her as a suspect in the murder of her own cousin.

"How are you holding up, kid?" Mindy asked. Even though she was just three years older than Dana, she had referred to her as "kid," since Dana was the new kid on the block.

"I feel like the elephant man around here, I'm this close to shouting, 'I am not an animal,'" Dana said, holding her index finger and thumb close together to illustrate to Mindy how close she was from losing it.

"Hang in there, kid. This is nothing but a rough start. You will be fine and you will thrive here once this murder business is concluded and the gossip brigade moves on to something new to gossip about," Mindy said, handing Dana a latte and sesame bagel with mango cream cheese. The bagel and cream cheese were both made in-house.

Dana joined Courtney on the beach. Despite having brought two beach chairs down from the house, Courtney was lying on a large blue and gold Golden State Warriors beach towel she had carefully laid out on the sand.

"How are you doing, sweetie?" Courtney asked.

Dana laughed. "Mindy asked me the same question," she said.

"Well, we're worried about you. This has been a stressful few days," Courtney said.

"I know. Thanks. That's why I need for today to be just a normal, hanging out on the beach, relax, have fun, normal day," Dana said.

"You got it," Courtney winked.

Dana and Courtney had been lying out on the beach for about an hour when they heard that Kansas surfer in his California surfer accent shout out at them, "Pura vida, ladies."

Dana and Courtney looked up and saw Big Mike waving as he clopped like a Clydesdale on the beach.

He was in his typical uniform, blue and red board shorts with white stars on the blue section of the shorts and a white tank top shirt.

"Ladies? Moi?" Courtney said as she and Dana broke out laughing.

"Hi, Big Mike. How are you?" Dana said. She appreciated that Big Mike, along with Mindy, was one of the few persons in the community that did not treat Dana like she was radioactive.

"I'm doing gnarly...another day in paradise," he said, looking out into the water.

"All right, go dubs," Big Mike said, pointing at Courtney's Golden State Warriors beach towel. He squatted down so he could talk at eye level with them. "What's cooking?" he asked.

Dana and Courtney both laughed out loud.

Big Mike smiled wide. "What did I miss?" he said, joining them in laughter.

"You're the third person in the last hour to ask me how I'm doing," Dana explained their outburst.

"It's a good thing to have people that care about you," Big Mike said, sounding the most serious Dana had ever heard him talk.

"It is. Thank you for asking. I'm doing just fine," Dana said.

"How about some surfing lessons? Get your mind off the bad stuff. On the house," Big Mike said.

"We couldn't accept that," Dana said.

"Nonsense. I have Julio watching the shop; I was already going to go surfing, so just tag along. I can use the practice teaching for the tourists," Big Mike said.

"Aren't we tourists?" Dana asked.

"No way, dude, you have moved down here full time, you're no tourist," Big Mike said, standing back up.

"Where do you surf?"

"It's about a ten-minute drive from here. Best breaks in the province for beginners. Nice and smooth," Big Mike said.

Dana and Courtney looked at each other and shrugged.

It was the type of impulsive thing that Dana would have never done in her life without research, planning, and over-thinking it to death.

"Let's go," Dana said, getting to her feet and wiping sand from her body.

Dana had surfed as a teenager growing up in the Bay Area, but the waters of the Pacific in Northern California were too cold for her taste and she hated wearing a wetsuit. It had been over fifteen years since she last surfed. Michigan born and raised Courtney had never surfed, even though they would see surfers at Ocean Beach in San Francisco or off of Highway One between San Francisco and Half Moon Bay. She kept telling Dana for the last decade that *someday* she would try surfing.

"Today is that day," Dana told her.

Big Mike had an old, beat-up Toyota pickup truck, crammed with surfboards and boogie boards in its bed. Dana climbed in first. It was a tight fit in the pickup's cab with Big Mike behind the wheel, Dana in the middle, and Courtney hanging out the window, since Big Mike had informed them once on the road that the air conditioner on the truck stopped working ten years ago.

"What happened there?" Dana asked, pointing at the empty slot where the radio should be.

"After they stole it a third time, I got the hint," Big Mike said. He didn't sound upset, but amused. "Such is life in the tropics."

Dana and Courtney spent two hours surfing with Big Mike. It was a blast. It surprised Dana what a good teacher Big Mike was. He appeared to be a flakey, unreliable goof-off who probably smoked too much of the funny stuff, but he turned very professional when it came to the surfing lesson. "You have to respect her," Big Mike kept saying—"her" being the ocean.

After surfing, they stopped at a beach shack, where Dana ate one of the most delicious fish tacos she had ever eaten.

Big Mike shared how much he liked Uncle Blake.

"An old hippie, that one," he had said, laughing.

"Did he ever say that he wanted to sell Casa Verde?" Dana asked.

"Oh, no way, man. He loved Casa Verde. Built that house from scratch. Not that he didn't get offers all the time," Big Mike said.

"Really? From whom?" Dana asked.

"Well, multiple offers from the same man," Big Mike said.

"Let me guess, Gustavo Barca?" Dana asked.

"Barca indeed. He's been after your property for a long, long time. Shady stuff. Especially once your uncle fell ill and moved back to the States. He was like a shark having picked up the scent of blood," Big Mike said, sounding sad.

"It's a beautiful country with beautiful people, but like any place, there are some bad apples rotting the lot. Gustavo Barca is rot," Big Mike continued.

After their late lunch of fish tacos, gallo pinto, and pineapple juice, they headed back to Mariposa Beach.

"Thanks, Big Mike, it was nice to just have fun today," Dana said as he dropped them off at Casa Verde.

"Anytime, amiga. See you around. And be careful with that big bad wolf up there," Big Mike said, pointing towards the footpath leading up to Gustavo Barca's resort.

Big Mike drove off in his pickup truck.

Later that day, Dana was waiting for Benny to arrive at seven o'clock that night. He had been having dinner with Dana and Courtney every night, and sometimes also lunch and breakfast.

"I'm feeling like a third wheel," Courtney said, watching Dana get dressed.

"What are you talking about? He's my lawyer. It's like a business dinner."

"Uh-huh. That's why you're spending all that time getting ready?" Courtney said.

"The last thing I need right now is to get involved with a man. Especially my lawyer," Dana said, her voice cracking a bit.

"Maybe when all this legal stuff is resolved. You deserve to be happy," Courtney said.

Dana managed a smile. *Maybe*, she thought.

Benny arrived on time as usual. When Dana was researching for information about living in Costa Rica, she noticed a lot of warnings online about tico time—used regarding the tardiness and general lack of being on time that supposedly afflicted the Costa Rican populace, but not Benny. He was as reliable as a Swiss watch.

He had his laptop bag slung over his shoulder. He seemed to be more in business mode than ever before, having spent the previous day in San José.

When he saw Dana, though, he smiled warmly. She liked that.

"What did you two do today? Staying out of trouble, I hope," Benny said. He had begged Dana not to go out snooping around and stepping on Agent Picado's toes.

"We were good, we lay out on the beach and took surfing lessons over at Playa Brava with Big Mike," Dana said.

"Nice guy. He's quite the character. A throwback to the old-school surfer dudes that used to visit Costa Rica back in the seventies and eighties," Benny said.

"Yes, he is. We had fun. He said he was pretty friendly with Uncle Blake. Shared some nice stories. He told me that Gustavo Barca offered to buy his property several times," Dana said.

Benny nodded. "Your uncle threw out one of Barca's representatives who kept badgering him to sell. And when your uncle was sick and went back to the States, Barca put up the pressure to get him to sell Casa Verde. Your uncle's illness was like chum in the water to Barca," Benny said.

"What a jerk," Dana said.

"Real estate people love the big two Ds," Benny said.

"What are those?"

"Death and divorce. The two Ds are good for business," Benny said.

"That's terrible," Dana said, realizing how true that statement was. Her divorce led to the sale of the house she and her ex-husband had shared. He then bought a new house for his new wife. The new wife had sold her house to move into their new home.

Had Dana not inherited Casa Verde, she would have bought her own place. That's four real estate transactions right there off of one divorce. Toss in the legal fees being racked up over the property dispute with Roy and Skylar, and now she was keeping lawyers fat and happy.

Benny could see that running the tally in her head.

"Amazing, isn't it?" he said, jarring Dana out of that thought.

"Yeah, I hadn't thought about it that way, but that's just sad," Dana said.

Benny brought steaks he called lomito, thin cuts of beef that he had marinated overnight with onion, garlic, and Salsa Lizano —a Worcestershire-like sauce found in nearly every Costa Rican home, restaurant, and roadside food stand.

Benny fired up the Weber gas grill that was in the backyard and smiled. "I figured Ramón would make sure the propane tank was filled."

Benny grilled the steaks to perfection. They ate the lomito with a side of white rice, a repollo which was a tangy and crunchy salad made of thinly sliced cabbage, diced tomatoes, onions, jalapeño, chopped cilantro, and topped with fresh lime juice from limes picked from the trees on the Casa Verde property, as were the fried yucca fries which had been cut, peeled, and chopped by Ramón from the yucca roots out back.

"This is so delicious. I didn't know you could cook," Dana said.

"I enjoy it, but don't get to do much cooking with my busy practice, so I indulge in it when I'm down here, since things aren't as hectic as when I'm in San José," Benny explained, smiling.

After dinner, they chatted but didn't talk much about the

murder or the legal wrangling, and Dana thought that it was sublime. The day with Big Mike, the nice dinner. This was what she had envisioned when moving down to Blue Butterfly Beach, not dealing with a murder and legal matters.

"When are you going back to San Francisco?" Benny asked Courtney.

"I'm supposed to go next week, but I'm not leaving Dana in this chaos and with a killer out there on the loose," Courtney replied.

Dana felt relieved to hear Courtney say that, but she also felt selfish and guilty for wanting her to stay for as long as possible. Dana knew that Courtney had a job to go back to with an employer who would not be too keen if she wasn't back to work on the expected day.

"You can always tell your boss that you need to stay longer because you're helping your best friend during a nasty legal dispute with her cousin who was murdered in Costa Rica and she's a prime suspect. How could they say no to that request?"

"Don't come back. That's what they would say," Courtney said, laughing.

Dana was being morbid, but she found that humor was a great way to deal with such unpleasantry.

TWENTY-SEVEN

The next morning, Dana lowered Big Red's soft top down, as usual, and Courtney sat next to her in the passenger seat, as usual.

They were at the front gate when they saw Ramón hunched over a weed whacker, tinkering with it.

Dana stopped the jeep and leaned out the driver's side and she called out in Spanish, "Hi Ramón, is that machine giving you problems?"

"Not really. It's just an old machine that jams up a lot. But I can fix it. I always fix it," he said proudly.

"We're going up to Nosara to do some grocery shopping," Dana said.

"Ah, the big town," Ramón said. Dana smiled. Nosara's population was just under six thousand, so compared to tiny Mariposa Beach, it was the big town. Nosara even had a traffic light.

Ramón said he needed nothing, so Dana made her way out the front gate and slammed on the accelerator, kicking up dust and gravel as Big Red took off.

"Oh, jeez, not again. Please slow down, and no more made-up shortcuts through rivers this time!" Courtney demanded as she grabbed the passenger's side grab handle of the jeep, or as she began to call it, the *hold on for your dear life* handle.

Dana drove to the pueblo side of Nosara, where they had spotted Skylar and Barca. They were going to the supermarket where everything was tico-priced, so about half the price of grocery stores in the tourist part of town.

Supermercado El Rey, which in English translates to Super-market The King, was the largest grocery town in the Nosara district.

The locals, who were used to tourists and expats not speaking the language, appreciated Dana's excellent Spanish.

Courtney just nodded and smiled, not understanding a word being said between Dana and the stock boy. Courtney took Spanish in high school and thought she could handle it, but in the rapid pace of the native speakers, they might as well have been speaking Chinese or some other language she didn't understand.

It impressed her how well Dana could speak it and hold her own.

"He said these are fresh pineapples from a nearby farm," Dana said. She carefully placed two pineapple plants into her shopping cart.

About thirty minutes later, they left the grocery store with a cart full of groceries. A teenager working for the grocery store would not take no for an answer when he began to push the cart with four full grocery bags outside. Dana looked at Courtney and shrugged. The kid put the bags in the back of Big Red. He smiled widely at the tip Dana gave him and sauntered back inside.

Dana took out some money for a kid who told Dana he would keep an "ojo" on the jeep as he pointed to his right eye, meaning he would watch the parked jeep for her while she was inside, shopping.

"You think that's really necessary here? We've shopped at that sketchy Safeway on Market Street at midnight," Courtney said with a laugh.

"It's not that much money, and I might as well play it safe with Big Red," Dana said as she smiled at the kid and agreed to his offer.

"I think you're falling big for Big Red," Courtney said with a laugh.

The kid was there when they came out. He stood next to Big Red, standing proudly as if to say, *See, it's still here and not a scratch on it.* Dana gave him his tip. He smiled approvingly at the amount as he ran to the street to stop traffic, then he waved Dana onto the street and waved goodbye as she drove away.

On the way out of town, Dana pulled over to the side of the dusty road and parked in front of a friendly-looking old man dressed in his campesino garb who sat next to a larger cooler with a sign that read, *Agua De Pipa Fría.*

"Oh, that sounds good right about now, it's so hot," Dana said, pointing at the old man.

"What's he selling?" Courtney asked, not understanding the sign.

"Agua de pipa fría means cold coconut water," Dana explained.

Courtney lit up. "Oh, I love coconut water."

Dana got out of Big Red as the old man jumped out of his shaded lawn chair. Dana ordered two pipas. He bent down to his cooler and plopped it open. Dana looked down and saw that it was packed full of coconut shells buried in ice.

"Um, what's that?" Courtney said.

"Oh, this isn't that fancy-schmancy eight-dollar coconut

water we get back home in a container. This is one hundred percent the real thing," Dana said, smiling.

She laughed watching Courtney's reaction as the old man removed two unhusked coconut shells from the ice. He placed one shell on the edge of a wooden stump, then he pulled out a machete and whacked at the shell a few times until he had carved a hole in the shell's top so he could put a straw into it, and handed her the chilled coconut shell.

"Thank you." Dana took a sip from the straw. "Oh, man, this is so good."

The old man did the same thing to Courtney's shell. Her first sip was hesitant, like a child being forced to eat broccoli, then her eyes widened. "Oh my, this is delicious!"

Dana paid the old man, and they sat inside Big Red, drinking the delicious coconut water right from the shell, when a vehicle suddenly veered off from the main road and parked right behind them as it kicked up dust and gravel. They were sitting in the jeep with the top down, so the dust engulfed both of them, much to Dana's annoyance.

"Who the heck is that?" Courtney asked, looking back at the car.

"I guess someone really wants some coconut water." Dana watched the car door open and out stepped Detective Gabriela Rojas.

Dana tensed up and almost spat out her coconut water, expecting to see Picado exit next, but Rojas was by herself.

For a moment, Dana envisioned a scene from TV and the movies where the cops swarm out of their cars to arrest someone. She felt that momentary panic that they would arrest her and she would be on a real-life version of the *Locked Up Abroad* television show.

"Sorry for kicking up all this dust, I was heading out of town when I saw you from the corner of my eye and I just pulled the wheel. I wanted to talk to you," Rojas said.

"What about?" Dana asked nervously.

"First, relax. I know you didn't kill your cousin, and Picado holds details of the cases he leads close to the vest even from me, but I'm sure he's ruled you out, but he wants to leave you off balance, so he won't officially rule you out," Rojas said.

"What's his problem with me?"

"Don't take it so personally. He gets his kicks by making foreigners, especially from the U.S., feel afraid of him. And he said you're too nosey. Interfering in the investigation, so he believes you need to be taught a lesson."

"It's easier said than done not to take things personally when you're accused of murder," Dana said.

"You haven't been accused of anything. We were just doing routine background checks on everyone in Roy's orbit," Rojas said.

"You checked me up in the States?"

Rojas nodded. "FBI and SFPD. It took a few calls, but they were helpful."

"You find anything good?" Dana asked. She was genuinely curious.

Rojas smiled. "Aside from parking tickets and blowing off jury duty, you came back squeaky clean," Rojas replied.

Dana blushed. Parking tickets were normal in San Francisco, but ignoring her jury summons made her feel ashamed.

Courtney said, "I told you ignoring that jury duty summons would come back to haunt you."

"I was planning to take care of that, but then I was moving down here..." Dana began to explain, but Rojas interrupted her by laughing.

"We don't have juries made up of regular citizens in Costa Rica. If we did, we wouldn't be able to get any of them to show up for jury duty, even if we threatened them with death," Rojas said, laughing.

"I still feel guilty about it."

"Don't worry, we won't extradite you for that, so you can stay down here in hiding," Rojas said, teasing.

"Gee, thanks. How about making it official that I'm no longer a suspect in my cousin's murder to boot?" Dana asked.

"Sorry. That's up to Picado. I think he's enjoying making you squirm, but I'm going to tell you something because I think you need to know. And I told Picado that you should know, but he disagreed with me and he's the boss. If he finds out I'm talking to you off the record like this, he'll have a coronary from a fit of rage, and when they paddle him back to life, he'll make sure I lose my job. So please, aside from the three of us here, don't tell anyone about what I'm going to share with you, okay?" Rojas asked.

"Of course, you can count on it," Dana said.

Courtney added, "I won't say a word."

Rojas looked at Dana and said, "Not even to your good-looking lawyer friend."

"Benny?" Dana asked, sounding incredulous.

"Yes, Benny Campos."

Dana felt her stomach tighten. She had planned to tell him about running into and talking with Rojas.

"Okay, but why?" Dana asked.

"Because I don't trust him," Rojas said.

Dana recoiled at the thought of not being able to trust Benny. He had proved himself to be a good friend and a good lawyer, so what could Rojas have on him that she didn't trust him?

"May I ask why you don't trust him?" Dana asked.

"For one, he's a lawyer. I don't like lawyers. Second, he's the attorney on record for your property and he'll make a heck of a lot more money if Skylar successfully contests your uncle's will and she sells the land to Gustavo Barca. With you he'll just get nominal fees for paperwork and legal advice here and there. With Skylar and Barca, he'll rack up huge legal fees."

Dana was stunned. She hadn't thought about that possibility. Rojas must have noticed Dana's face suddenly turn ashen. "Hey, my job makes me suspicious about everyone's motives. It doesn't mean I'm right. I'm just answering your question."

"It's okay. I trust Benny, but you're right, and I hadn't thought about that possibility. I will keep what you're going to tell me just between us three. I won't tell Benny."

Rojas nodded approvingly. "We haven't found the murder weapon yet, but the forensic team said it was a serrated knife; likely a steak knife. So we checked with the resort, since that's where your cousin was staying, and the forensics team took some samples back to San José for testing. It took them a couple days, but the medical examiner just confirmed that the wounds on your cousin's body match the knives that were taken from the resort for testing. The resort uses a very fancy type of knife from Switzerland that has the resort's logo carved into the blade which matched the wounds, so now we know where the killer got his or her weapon," Rojas explained.

It has to be Skylar, Dana thought.

"So that's great news, right? It helps you narrow things down," Dana asked.

"It helps, but on the night of the murder, there were close to two hundred guests at the resort, plus a staff of fifty-two. Any of them had access to one of those knives, so that's a lot of possible suspects, and a defense attorney would have a field day with it. Add to the mix a lot of rich, powerful, VIP tourists and locals that stay at the resort, which puts pressure on us so we have to walk on eggshells when it comes to interviewing any of those VIP guests."

"Too bad I'm not VIP so Picado had to walk on eggshells around me."

Rojas smiled. "In your favor is that you hadn't been to the resort, until after the murder, so it would have been more difficult for you, although not impossible, to get one of those distinctive knives to kill your cousin. So that puts Skylar back at the top of the list of suspects. I know you don't get along or hang out with Skylar, but be very careful and do not let her near you, especially alone. We should have enough evidence to arrest her soon, but Picado really wants to find that knife, so until Skylar is under arrest, I recommend you stay put in Casa Verde."

Dana thanked the detective for the warning and left, heading back to town.

Dana pulled into her driveway as the green gate closed behind her. Courtney looked back to make sure it closed. Dana was having visions of a knife-wielding Skylar coming up the driveway.

She parked Big Red, and they got out.

"That's it. We must stay put now until they arrest that crazy nut job," Courtney said.

Dana gave her a noncommittal nod.

"Dana!"

Back in the house, Dana went to the book nook while Courtney took a bath. She sat at Blake's old writing desk. She looked around and sighed. She had began the daunting task of sorting through the thousands of books which she had scattered higgledy-piggledy across the floor. Wally sauntered into the room, checking out the mess. She swore she heard him tsk.

"It's okay, kitty, I'll get this mess sorted soon enough," Dana said.

Wally meowed, rubbed his body against her leg, and then sat on guard, his tail wrapped around his paws. Dana was looking at Wally being protective when she noticed, for the first time, a rolling whiteboard that was tucked away in a corner.

Under Wally's watchful eyes, Dana wheeled it out to the center of the room. There were three markers—two black, one red—and an eraser on the whiteboard's tray. Dana picked up the black one; she removed its cap and sniffed it. It smelled like it still had some ink left. She then tested it on the whiteboard, and to her surprise, it worked. After at least three years of sitting there untouched, she was sure the markers would have been dried out. She took the eraser to get rid of the test squiggly line she had drawn and she went to work.

She wrote SUSPECTS at the top of the board and underlined it, then she began to map out what she had in her head.

Thirty minutes later, she heard Courtney calling for her.

"I'm in the library," Dana called out, rousing Wally from a deep sleep. He had crashed out on a pile of books. He got up, stretched, yawned, and bolted from the room as if he had seen a ghost.

"Weirdo," Dana said with a chuckle.

"I thought you snuck...What are you doing?" Courtney said, looking at the whiteboard.

"My suspects," Dana said, looking at her handiwork.

"Okay, newsflash, you're not a detective. You don't have any suspects," Courtney said.

"Check it out," Dana said, ignoring what she said. "We all know that Skylar is at the top of the list, but we also have Gustavo Barca, who might have gotten wind of Roy waffling about contesting the will now that he and Marisol were in love. I doubt he would get his hands dirty, but he has the connections and money to hire a killer."

"Dana..."

She continued talking, "But I started to think that it makes little sense that Barca would hire a professional who would then use a steak knife from his resort, putting him in the crosshairs of the police. So that makes this more of a passion thing, so that's why I put Marisol Arias second on the list. Think about it. I don't know her from Adam, so for all I know she puts on this soul mate routine for me when, in reality, Roy meets up with her at the resort. He dumps her, she goes into a rage because she thinks they are soul mates, so she picks up the steak knife, and boom, kills him."

"And then she drags him all the way down the footpath? She weighs like a hundred pounds soaking wet," Courtney said.

"Yeah, I thought about that too. But maybe she took the steak knife earlier and had it in her bag."

"I don't know. And why on Earth is Claudio's name up there?" Courtney asked.

"He, more than anyone, would have easy access to the resort cutlery. He hates his boss, and Barca, who is not only a terrible employer, but he's trying to take his grandmother and his parents' home. He knows that if Roy is dead and the legal case ends, that I won't sell to Barca and his family's homes are safe. That's a huge motive."

"Okay, that all makes sense, but what are you going to do? Go all Jessica Fletcher and go catch a dangerous killer? Just leave it to the cops. I'm sure they've come up with these same scenarios as you have. I'm going to make us some daiquiris so we can chill out and stop thinking about murder," Courtney said as she turned and walked out of the library.

Dana looked at her whiteboard. "I hope Picado is looking at these suspects too," she said out loud to an empty room.

TWENTY-EIGHT

Dana adhered to Detective Rojas's advice to stay home. Benny was in San José, so she wouldn't see him for a few days. Then Courtney went on a daiquiri-making spree. They drank cocktails while playing cards and watching a couple movies on Netflix on her laptop. She woke up in the morning with a daiquiri-induced headache and blamed Courtney for it. She was sure her friend wanted to get her woozy with rum to keep from snooping, and the plan had worked like a charm. But now her head was paying the price.

She took a long, hot shower, then dressed in an orange San Francisco Giants T-shirt and her khaki cargo shorts. Wally lifted his head up from the bed briefly to see what was going on before plopping it back down and going back to sleep.

Courtney was still sleeping, so Dana left her a note that she was headed out to get some coffee and bagels from Mindy's place and would be right back.

She drove down to Ark Row and parked in front of Mindy's cafe. It was early, and there weren't many people around, so she jumped when she heard a horn honk. She turned to see Felicia

Banks pull into the parking spot right next to her in the sporty Audi Q2.

Dana sighed. The last thing she wanted to do before coffee was fend off the pushy real estate agent once again.

"I've been looking for you," Felicia said, hopping out of the car.

"Oh, why is that?" Dana asked.

Felicia seemed in a hurry, and she seemed frazzled in a black T-shirt and black sweatpants, not her usual stylish attire.

"Everything okay?"

"Yes, sorry to bug you like this, but I really need to talk to you," Felicia said, pulling strands of blonde hair from her face. She was chewing on a large wad of bubble gum that made her thick Boston accent even more difficult for Dana to understand her.

"If this is about selling or renting out Casa Verde, I'm not interested."

"No, it's not about that. I have some information about your cousin's murder and about Skylar. I think I can prove she did it."

That got Dana's attention.

"What?"

"It's very sensitive information. I live just down the street. Let's go to my place to talk in private. It's not as good as Mindy's, but I have coffee brewing," Felicia said.

"Have you talked to the police about any of this?" Dana asked.

"No, especially since it involves you and your land, so I wanted to talk to you first, as a courtesy. Ask Benny to come along, since he's your lawyer."

"He's in San José."

From her facial expression, it seemed Felicia was happy to learn that.

Dana still thought this was a ploy to talk her into selling, but her curiosity got the best of her. What information did she have? So she got into Felicia's car. It was a nice and fancy car but too cramped for her taste, especially for what was supposed to be an SUV.

Felicia drove away from Ark Row and off Main Street as they headed away from Mariposa Beach.

"I thought you lived in town?" Dana asked.

"No, I'm just right outside of town. Like Benny," Felicia said.

"Well, this is pretty private now, what is it?" Dana asked.

"I've been working with Roy and Skylar for the last two years as the go-between between them and Gustavo Barca. That deal with Mr. Barca, I set it up. Roy had assured me he would inherit Casa Verde when his father died. It made sense to me since he was his only child, so when that didn't happen and you came into the picture, I'm the one who convinced Gustavo Barca to pay for them to fight you for the property. I'm sorry, I know it's crappy, but my commission upon the sale of the property to Mr. Barca would be huge, the biggest of my career. I wouldn't have to peddle Airbnb rentals anymore, so I've been advising Roy and Skylar...Well, now just Skylar," Felicia said as she drove.

Dana was stunned. "I didn't see your name mentioned in any of the paperwork regarding Casa Verde."

"I have a signed agreement with Roy and Skylar, which I had amended with Skylar after Roy's death. The real estate disclosure laws in Costa Rica aren't as restrictive as they are back in the States, and all my business dealings are through a company I set up just for this deal, so my name will never be attached to any of these dealings. I know it sounds shady to you, but it's all legit," Felicia said.

Dana wasn't so sure.

"So why are you telling me all of this now? You've been

helping them make my life quite miserable these past few months."

Felicia pulled into a driveway. Like Casa Verde, there was a tall wall surrounding it and a big black metal gate. The wall and gate were much bigger than Casa Verde. Dana assumed the home on the other side of that wall would be quite bigger and more luxurious than her home. Felicia pressed on a gate remote opener.

As they waited for the gate to open, Felicia turned to look at Dana. "I might be ruthless in business. I won't make any apologies for that. When a man is shrewd and cutthroat in business, he's admired. But a woman...well, you know what they call us. But when it comes to murder, I will not be a party to that. Skylar told me everything that happened the night of Roy's murder, and you're now in grave danger, and I'm terrified I'll be next because I know too much."

The gate finally opened and Felicia drove onto the property as the big gate closed shut behind them. Dana was still reeling about everything Felicia had said, but she was taken aback at the stunningly beautiful, large, three-story home in front of her.

"This is your house?" Dana asked.

Felicia ignored the question and said, "Let's go inside. Once I tell you everything, we can call Detective Picado."

She parked, and they walked inside the house. The front entrance was actually the top floor of the house. It was an open space like a loft, but it was palatial.

Dana looked down below and she could see lower floors along with a wraparound staircase. It felt like she was standing at the top deck of a cruise ship.

There was a beautiful large bar carved from the exotic woods that looked like the one Dana had seen at the resort.

It was a full bar like you would find at a business, not a

private home. Behind it were large floor-to-ceiling windows with panoramic views of the Pacific Ocean in the distance.

There was a half-empty bottle of Glenlivet 18-Year-Old Single Malt Scotch on the bar next to an empty glass. Dana could see that the glass had been recently used, which struck her as odd at seven in the morning.

Felicia walked up to the bar. She removed the big blob of chewed-up gum from her mouth and put it into a napkin. She then poured herself a drink.

"He always has the good stuff," she said as she held up the glass and downed it like it was a shot of tequila. She winced, then she poured herself another drink. "Can I get you a drink?"

"Um, no thank you. It's seven in the morning, Felicia," Dana said.

Felicia shrugged. "This is like my fourth drink already, or maybe it's my fifth, I've lost track."

Dana looked around at the posh home and thought there was no way this was Felicia's house.

"You said *he always has the good stuff*, who is he?" Dana asked.

"Gustavo Barca, of course. Honey, you think I could afford a place like this with the pittance I make? I still haven't recovered from the real estate meltdown of two thousand seven to two thousand nine. You thought it was bad in the States, you should have seen what it did to the Costa Rican real estate market, especially my specialty selling homes to Americans. As they say, when the United States catches a cold, the rest of the world gets pneumonia. Well, I got it bad, and I've barely recovered," Felicia said. She downed the drink in one gulp and slammed the glass on the bar's counter.

"What's going on, Felicia? Why did you bring me here?"

"Because of Skylar, I told you."

"What about Skylar?"

"She's here," Felicia said, slurring her words and giggling.

"I'm leaving," Dana said, turning towards the door.

"How are you going to get back, silly?"

"I'll walk."

"Wait, wait, we'll get the whole truth from Skylar herself. She right in there," Felicia said as she walked towards a closed door.

Dana watched her as she opened the door and went inside. "Come on, get up," Dana heard Felicia saying, but she couldn't see what was going on inside the room.

A moment later, Felicia walked out of the room with Skylar, whom she had gagged with duct tape over her mouth and had restrained her arms behind her back. Felicia shoved her from behind. That's when Dana noticed she was holding a gun.

Dana took a step back and Felicia pointed the gun at her.

"You're not going anywhere, troublemaker," she said.

Crap. Dana froze. She could tell that Skylar had been crying. Her eyes and face were red and puffy.

"What are you doing, Felicia?"

"In the real estate business, we call it a 'commissionectomy.' It's when a real estate agent does everything they can to save a commission from going down the toilet. I've been working this deal for two years and I'm not letting it go down the toilet because of you. So sit down," Felicia said as she pointed to a large sectional couch with the gun.

Dana did as she was told and sat down. Felicia then shoved Skylar, who fell on the couch next to Dana.

Skylar began crying. The duct tape muffled her cries and whimpering over her mouth. It was a side of the usually fiery tomcat that Dana had never seen before, but then again, she had seen no one tied up, gagged, and held at gunpoint before. She had never had a gun pointed at her. And she didn't like it one bit, especially since it was obvious that Felicia was drunk and was waving that gun around like it was a toy.

Dana was calm. And it surprised her that was staying calm under the dire circumstances. She felt anger at the whole situation.

"So you're going to kill us both for a commission?" Dana asked.

"It's an enormous commission," Felicia said, sounding almost offended at the question.

"You killed Roy," Dana said.

Felicia smiled. She walked over to the bar, still pointing the gun in Dana and Skylar's direction. She reached behind the bar and removed a plastic bag with a big steak knife inside. She put on latex gloves and removed the knife. She held it up so Dana could see it. The Tranquil Bay Resort logo was on the blade just as Detective Rojas had said.

"Why?"

"Because of you," Felicia seethed. "Two years I've worked on this deal. Putting up with Roy and Skylar's insufferable demands and, nonstop, day and night, whine, whine, whine, for *two years*. Shaking me down for money for this and that. And it was okay. I had the contract signed. I just had to wait for that idiot, Blake Kirkpatrick, to die. He held on way too long, but finally he died. Casa Verde would soon belong to Roy and the deal would go through, but no, Roy's such a piece of work that his own father cut him from the will. So I've been in commissionectomy mode ever since then," Felicia explained.

"So you were that anonymous buyer that approached Benny," Dana said.

"One of my many shell companies. All you had to do was accept my offer. But nope, you're going through some sort of mid-life crisis and you want to move down here and blow my deal. I would not let that happen, so I convinced Barca to bankroll Roy and Skylar so we can end up with the land. Then Roy starts to waffle. He's in love with a freaking yoga teacher. Can you believe that? Are you kidding me? So I have two idiotic cousins going through a mid-life crisis that will cost me hundreds of thousands of dollars, no way. So I figure with Roy out of the way, then I only have to deal with Skylar, who I know wants nothing more than to sell the land to Barca and leave the country. It was perfect," Felicia explained.

"But you wanted insurance, so you were going to plant that knife on me, that way they would arrest me for the murder, making it a certainty that Skylar would get Casa Verde," Dana said.

"Smart cookie, that one. Don't you agree?" Felicia said to the gagged Skylar. "Oops, sorry, you can't talk," she said, giggling drunkenly.

"I kept trying to get onto your property to plant the knife, but you wouldn't even take my calls, how rude by the way, you hurt my feelings," Felicia said mockingly.

"That simpleton Ramón was always there, so I couldn't sneak into Casa Verde. Bravo on your security. So that gave enough time for you and Picado to find out that Roy was in love and Barca tired of supporting Skylar. He told me the other night the odds of winning in court were slim to none and he was tired of supporting Skylar and putting up with her not so endearing personality, and to boot, his sources in the OIJ warned him that Skylar would soon be arrested for Roy's murder, so he was going to walk away from the whole bloody mess. So easy for him to walk away after all that time and money, he's a billionaire. It's just another blown deal to him. He gets to move on with life still stinking rich. But for me? It would ruin me."

"I don't get it," Dana said. "If Skylar was going to be arrested and charged with killing Roy, you would have gotten away with murder, scot-free. No one knew about your involvement."

"Did you not hear what I said? This blown deal would leave me destitute. I've been stealing from my clients to keep up my good life. But they will soon catch on. And I'll be worse than poor, I'll be in jail. I will not let that happen. Besides, I earned that money! It's my money. I've gone this far. I already killed Roy, so why not go a little further to make sure the deal goes through?" Felicia said.

"So you're going to kill us both, how is that going to save your sale?" Dana asked.

"Barca let Skylar stay here for a few days so she would be out of his hair while he made the arrangements to send her back to California. This is one of his many homes I manage, like a servant. Everyone knows how snoopy you are sticking your nose into Picado's case, so it won't surprise anyone that when you found out that Skylar was here, you drove out here in your jeep. We'll never know what went down, perhaps you were both in cahoots to kill poor Roy, but in the end, you kill Skylar with the same knife that killed Roy, but good old Skylar manages to shoot you with this gun Barca keeps at this house. You both die. I still have the signed contract with Roy and Skylar, so I have that covered, but why settle just for the commission? After all that hard work I've done and putting up with all the Kirkpatrick dysfunction, I deserve it all. So all I need for you to do is sign this new contract, where you're selling Casa Verde to me for a very favorable contract for deed which I've backdated. Barca's high-powered lawyers will make sure our contract is validated and I'm a millionaire by next summer. I have my eye on a lovely condo in Ibiza."

"Well, you've thought everything through, but if you're going to kill me, why on Earth would I sign your stupid contract for deed?" Dana said.

Felicia lost some of the smugness and bravado as she glared at Dana.

"Since the first day we met, I've always said that you talk too much," Dana said. She surprised herself on how she was handling everything with such confidence against someone who was planning to kill her.

Felicia stood in front of the couch with her back to the railing. She wobbled from the booze but she recovered and got into a shooting stance with both hands on the gun.

"Then I just kill you both because I can't stand either of you and then I disappear somewhere in Europe while I regroup. I actually like that idea even more. I'll be happily reliving killing three annoying Kirkpatricks."

Felicia cocked the revolver and pointed it at Dana. She glared at her and Dana realized what it meant when an evil person was said to have murder in their eyes. Suddenly Skylar sprung from the couch like a loose spring and she plowed into Felicia head first, shoving her back towards the banister. Dana watched in horror as Felicia screamed as she went over the railing and fell down below.

"Oh, no," Dana screamed as she ran to the edge just as Skylar's momentum was about to take her over the railing too. She had her hands tied, so she was helpless, but just as she was about to follow Felicia over the railing, Dana embraced Skylar in a bear hug and pulled back hard, falling onto the floor with Skylar landing on top of her. It hurt, but she was alive. And so was Skylar. Dana ignored the soreness and quickly got to her feet and looked over the railing down below to see what happened to Felicia. She had fallen three stories, landing on the very expensive, hard Italian marble floor.

She was dead.

EPILOGUE

The English and Spanish-language newspapers and television news channel went on a media feeding frenzy.

Casa Verde, Barca's home, and the footpath where Roy was killed, had become hot destinations for the macabre tourists.

The few days after everything went down between Dana, Skylar, and Felicia, things got so bad that Freddy Sanchez, the Tourist Police Officer, had to park his motocross bike in front of Casa Verde's front gate to keep the reporters and selfie-seeking onlookers out of the way and in check.

By the start of the second week after Felicia's death, everything had died down and interest in the case dwindled. Officer Freddy was back patrolling the beaches on his motorcycle and Dana finally could leave Casa Verde and go into town in peace.

"There she is!" Mindy had yelled out when Dana finally could make her way back to the coffee shop. "I'm not going to lie, all that attention was great for business! I might even go on vacation," Mindy joked after feeding the masses of police investigators, reporters, and looky-loos that had descended onto Mariposa Beach.

All the local merchants of Ark Row, although concerned for

what Dana had gone through, were happy at all the extra business Felicia's crime spree had brought to town. When pictures of Mariposa Beach's beautiful white sand and turquoise calm waters began to appear on the television news, websites, and in all the papers, new tourists began to arrive into town.

Claudio Villalobos even told Dana that since news of the crimes had been picked up by the cable news channels like CNN and other international news outlets like the BBC, they were now getting guests wanting to come to the luxurious resort they saw on the news.

"I guess there is no such thing as bad publicity," Dana had told Benny, amazed that the lurid details of what had happened had provided the little beach town a huge business boost.

"Silver linings, I guess," Benny said, equally perplexed at the post-crime events.

The OIJ forensics team from San José corroborated Dana and Skylar's version of the events after analyzing the tumble that Felicia Banks had taken to her death. The gun she had tried to use to kill Dana and Skylar landed on the floor below near her body.

Felicia's death was ruled self-defense, and they cleared both Skylar and Dana of any wrongdoing.

The blood on the knife that Felicia had shown Dana matched Roy Kirkpatrick's blood, so it was found to be the knife used to kill him, and Dana and Skylar were cleared from any involvement in Roy's murder.

It couldn't have been a cleaner way to wrap up the murder investigation for Detective Picado, not that he showed any relief or happiness about that. Even when he had officially cleared Dana, he did it with a scowl on his face and then he hightailed it back to Nicoya.

It overjoyed detective Rojas, who hugged Dana and wished her luck in her new hometown.

A few days later, Gustavo Barca sent a dozen yellow roses to Dana with a note that read:

"Dana, I'm glad you're okay. If you ever change your mind about selling Casa Verde, don't hesitate to call me. Regards, Gustavo."

"The nerve of that son of a biscuit, he just won't give up," Dana said incredulously.

"Those are beautiful flowers, though," Courtney said, smelling the roses.

Skylar had been shell-shocked after sending Felicia Banks over that railing. Once Felicia had fallen, Dana undid Skylar's restraints, and she had removed the duct tape from her mouth.

The two former enemies hugged and cried, and Dana thanked Skylar for saving her life and Skylar thanked her for stopping her from going over the railing too, thus saving her life as well.

It was an odd feeling that they had saved each other's lives. While they waited for the police to arrive, Dana had apologized for thinking she had killed Roy, and Skylar said the same thing.

As soon as Picado cleared Skylar, she left Costa Rica.

Once back in California, she dropped the case against Dana, believing the land to be a curse she wanted nothing to do with anymore. Dana imagined she was fine with collecting Roy's life insurance and moving on.

When Dana asked what she should do with Roy's body, Skylar told her that Roy had mentioned that he wanted to be cremated, but that she didn't care what Dana did with his body. She didn't want it.

Dana felt that was cold. It seemed old Skylar was getting back to normal.

So in keeping with Roy's wishes, as soon as the OIJ released his body to Dana, who was his next of kin in Costa Rica, she had him cremated. Since Skylar didn't want his ashes, Dana and

Benny put his ashes into a beautiful urn that they gave to a very grateful Marisol Arias.

Benny and Dana drove Courtney to the Juan Santamaría International Airport in Alajuela. Courtney had stayed on for another two weeks. Her boss was furious, so she wasn't sure if she had a job waiting for her back in San Francisco, but she couldn't leave Dana on her own dealing with the aftermath of one of the biggest crimes to hit the Costa Rican coast.

After tearful goodbyes and promises that they would visit each other in their respective home turfs, Courtney went through the security checkpoint at the terminal, disappearing into the passenger-only gate area of the airport.

It had been almost a week since Courtney went back to San Francisco, and although Dana missed her like crazy, she was glad to start her new life without all the drama of the past few weeks.

She had become closer to Mindy and had gone back to yoga, becoming friends with her new yoga teacher, Marisol Arias.

It had been a few days since she had seen Benny, who was back in San José at his law practice. She hated to admit it to herself, but she missed him a lot, and she wasn't sure how she felt about that. But she would worry about those feelings on another day.

Benny arrived right on time, as usual. They hugged. Dana felt it was an awkward hug.

Benny smiled wide, and he held her by the shoulders and said, "It's official, Casa Verde is yours, free and clear!"

At first, Dana gulped, thinking he was going for a kiss, and although she felt disappointment that he wasn't—*stop thinking about that*—Dana squealed with excitement over the good news and she hugged Benny again. This time it didn't feel awkward.

He pulled out a chilled bottle of champagne and two glasses. "This calls for some bubbly and a toast," Benny declared proudly as he twisted on the cork until it popped loudly as champagne gushed out like a geyser.

He poured the bubbly into the glasses.

"So now you can stay for sure," Benny said, smiling.

"I am," Dana said, tearing up.

"Have you given more thought to that business idea you mentioned?"

"You really think it's a good idea?" Dana asked.

"I think a bookstore is a wonderful idea, and we all know you have a lot of inventory," Benny said, pointing at the library with Uncle Blake's huge collection of paperbacks.

"Everything is going digital," Dana said. She was unsure if it made sense to open a bookstore.

"People love beach and pool reads, and the tablets and Kindles can be a pain, they can get wet, fried in the hot tropical sun, stolen, so people love paperbacks on the beach, and you would be the only English-language bookstore in the Nosara district. I think it's worth a shot," Benny said.

"I might just do it, then. But I need to mull it over more. For now, I want to celebrate this victory," Dana said, smiling.

Benny held up his glass of champagne and said, "Here's to you and your new home, Casa Verde."

Dana smiled. "Thanks to you and Uncle Blake, cheers."

"Ching, ching," Benny said as they clinked glasses.

Wally the cat waltzed in from around the corner and looked up at Dana and meowed his approval.

WHAT'S NEXT?

Dana Kirkpatrick is still a brand-spanking new ex-pat living in Mariposa Beach, Costa Rica so why not add new business owner into the mix?

She's busy opening the first and only bookstore in Mariposa Beach and worried about opening a brick and mortar business in the digital age but as a former newspaper reporter she has first-hand experience about working in a dying business. Besides, she loves books and challenges.

What she didn't count on was finding a dead body in her bookstore days before the grand opening.

Now the police are threatening to put the kibosh on the grand opening while they investigate and a pushy tourist seems a little too eager to get his hands on her second-hand books, but why?

Find out in the second book of the Costa Rica Beach Cozy Mystery Series, "A Book To Die For."

SNEAK PEEK OF A BOOK TO DIE FOR

After months of preparation, and a lot of the proverbial sweat, blood, and tears, the grand opening of Dana Kirkpatrick's bookstore was just days away but there was still a lot to do before then so she woke up earlier than usual to tackle her never-ending to-do list as soon as possible.

At five AM her iPhone alarm blasted a Luscious Jackson song waking her and Wally up.

Wally was Dana's cat, who had been sleeping at the bottom of the bed, curled up against her legs. Dana yawned and sat up looking down at the kitty who looked back at her with just one eye open. She laughed at the *what do you think you're doing this early* look he gave her.

"Good morning," she said to the cat.

Wally was not amused with her early morning cheeriness. Dana could almost swear that if he wasn't so comatose he would have hissed back.

"Hey don't give me that 'tude, I have a lot of stuff to do today. Grand opening is a few days away."

Wally plopped his tiny head back onto the bed. He yawned

and stretched while laying on his side. She wouldn't get any help from him.

"Bum," Dana said as she got out of bed.

To her surprise, Wally got up. "Oh, you are going to help? Good, because you need to get some practice at being the book-store cat."

Wally yawned for what must have been the fifth time but he tossed in a downward-facing dog yoga pose at the same time then he moseyed up to where Dana had been sleeping and he plopped down on the warm spot she had left behind and went back to sleep.

"Or not," Dana said chuckling as she made her way to the bathroom.

She brushed her teeth, washed her face and quickly got dressed. She glanced over at the bed as she slipped on her Rothy's slip-on flat shoes perfect for the busy day she had in front of her.

Wally was fast asleep again and didn't even bother to look up at her as she made her way out of the room. She gave him one more look over her shoulder. He was out cold.

"Bum," she said again making her way downstairs to the kitchen.

It was 5:12 AM. She grabbed a bag of fresh coffee beans from her friend Mindy's family farm in the Tarrazú region.

The beans had just been packed up a few days ago. *It doesn't get fresher than this*, Dana thought as she dumped a few spoonfuls of the deliciously smelling beans into a bean grinder. She hit the button, and the machine began to whirl and buzz at it ground up the beans.

She added water to the coffeemaker while the bean grinder did its thing. When the machine stopped making its racket, she took the container of freshly ground coffee and she put her nose in there like she was sniffing fine wine and took a deep inhale.

Smells so good she thought as she dumped the freshly ground coffee into the coffeemaker and hit the 'brew' button. Something she had done so often that the text on the button that once spelled 'brew' had long ago rubbed off.

While the coffee brewed, she ate a bowl of dry cereal and a banana handpicked from her backyard.

Less than ten minutes later with a large coffee tumbler in hand she climbed into Big Red—the nickname she had given to her cherry red vintage 1948 Jeep Willys—which was parked in her carport. She fired Big Red up and she made the quick drive from her place to Ark Row on Main Street where all the retail stores in town were located and where her soon-to-open bookstore would join the ark row.

It was about 5:35 AM and still pitch dark out when she parked in front. She had a heavy box of books that she had packed up the day before in the backseat so she would have to come back for the coffee tumbler full of that precious life-giving liquid.

She grabbed the box struggling to get a good grip on it. It was heavy, but she got a good hold of it as she made her way to her locked store.

At the front door, she hoisted the box onto a bent knee as she fidgeted around in her bag for the store's keys which seemed to think it would be fun to play a game of hide and seek as she tried to balance the heavy box on one knee.

"Dang it," she said, giving up the balancing act. She plopped the heavy box on the floor by her feet so she could focus on finding the illusive key.

"There you are you are, you little stinker," she said out loud into her purse as she pulled out the key.

She unlocked the overhead aluminum security drop-door and pushed it up until it rolled up into a tube. Now she had access the front door which she unlocked. She turned on the lights then went back outside and picked up the box of books which she brought inside and hoisted onto the counter.

She felt a strange energy that made the tiny brown hairs on her arm to stand at attention. She shrugged it off. It was early in the morning; dark and quiet — which causes the brain to interpret it as an ominous vibe.

"What you need is coffee," she said to herself, out loud. She began to head to the door in order go fetch her coffee tumbler from the jeep but that creepy vibe niggled at the back of her mind as she walked so she looked over her shoulder back towards the counter and she froze.

Did I just see what I saw?

She turned around to be sure taking a few steps towards the counter trying to convince herself that it was the darkness or the sleep in her eyes messing with her; making her see things that weren't there.

Too bad it wasn't just her mind playing tricks on her.

She wanted to scream but couldn't. She wanted to run outside but couldn't. Her feet felt like they were encased in two buckets of hardened cement.

She stood there for what seemed to be hours but it was just a moment or two as she stared down on the floor at the two feet sticking out from the other side of the counter.

Finally, her body released her mind from its stupor and she ran outside screaming.

What happens next?

Find out on October 6, 2019 when the second book in the Costa Rica Beach Cozy Mystery Series is published!

ABOUT K.C.

I was born and raised in Costa Rica, but now live in San Francisco, California. I've always loved cozy mysteries, so when I decided to write one, I just knew I had to base it in my home country of Costa Rica!

That's how this beach cozy mystery series came about. I'm excited to bring you more cozy mysteries set in the Pacific Coast of Costa Rica.

You can learn more about me and my books over at my website: www.KCAmes.com.

Sign up for my newsletter for book updates, animal pics, and my recipe book of traditional Costa Rica dishes, for free:

kcames.com/subscribe

Join my reader group on Facebook to make new friends:

kcames.com/group

Connect with me on social media...